SHIP OUT OF LUCK

THE ALICE LUCK SPACE ADVENTURES
BOOK 3

H. CLAIRE TAYLOR

ISBN: 978-1-959041-04-7 (H. Claire Taylor)

FFS Media, LLC

www.ffs.media

contact@hclairetaylor.com

PROLOGUE

There was this guy named Betty. She was only a guy in the gender-neutral sense of the word, which most of the multiverse uses without a second thought, because she was technically the egg-bearer of her species. This guy didn't use any of her eggs, though. She kept them for herself and discarded them as she pleased.

She was a wife at one point but had used her six legs, seven arms, and big fucking pincer to escape that nightmare, and now she was one of the revered Lexicographers.

None of them knew this guy was a female. It almost goes without saying that if they'd found out, they would've launched her into a black hole. (There is a strong correlation between having sperm and acting irrationally, but science has never found one-to-one biological causation for this.)

Lucky for Betty, the Lexicographers were a motley bunch, and no two were of the same species. It was rare to find two from the same star system. So, the only way to know the sex of the creature beside you in the

Lexicographer symposium cave was to ask, and no one had ever asked Betty. Instead, they had assumed by her name that she was a male, because Betty is usually short for Bettamolllamu, which is obviously masculine.

On this particular day, this guy, Betty, had something important to say. People who've had to hide who they are usually do.

She had called the assembly because, taking up the mantle of her long-dead brethren Dale, Hammy, Garbob, Vince, and Jimjam (not their real names), her pursuit for the name of the guy who was responsible for everything and nothing had finally turned up a fresh result.

Once Betty had settled on the premise that the first two letters of the name truly were HH, she proceeded to formulate the next one in her free time. She found she had a lot of free time now that she was not a wife. Sure, sometimes she had to pack up and move to another part of the galaxy when she sensed a supernova about to explode (old habits of wifery die hard), but she required very little food, as most things with exoskeletons do, and math didn't pay enough for her to own many things, so tidying took all of three minutes a day. That left her with quite a bit of time in her burrow to calculate.

The previous presentations of letters were now legend among the Lexicographers. The first, she'd heard, was presented with a projector on the cave walls, the second in an unnecessary 3D holographic form. If she were to get any respect at all beyond people calling her "this guy," she had to top those.

"Bring in the slaves," she said, scurrying down the steps of the semicircular auditorium toward center stage.

A side door opened and three naked and chained

beings stumbled through, as if shoved from behind. The onlookers gasped.

Not because of the slavery thing—they were unfortunately cool with that concept—but because of who the slaves were.

Never before had *Homo sapiens* set foot upon hallowed Lexicographer ground. The idea was repugnant to most, even in the context of slavery. (*Perhaps especially in that context,* you think. But again, slavery wasn't a big deal to these guys so long as they were not the slaves. However, it's safe to assume they'd start caring if they became slaves.)

"What do you think you're doing?" shouted a halibut-looking motherfucker from the middle of the spectators.

But Betty hadn't engaged her translating software, and since using the common tongue of English to better communicate had long ago been rejected by this group, she had no idea what the fish guy was saying. It had been an intentional choice not to activate her translating software for this. She didn't want to get psyched out. So long as the rest of the group used their tech, though, that was what mattered.

The slaves trudged forward in their shackles, all fleshy shades of brown and shivering. They were taller than most sentient beings, which only served to make their naked bodies appear lanky and awkward as they shuffled toward Betty. She'd already given them their orders ahead of time, and they knew the consequences if they failed to hit their cue.

Keeping their gaze on the floor, they listened attentively, as you can only when your sympathetic nervous system is on high alert, while she began her presentation.

"I have discovered the third letter in the name of that force that is everywhere and nowhere, the reason your wife left you."

From the crowd: "You smelly turd! How do you even know there *is* a third letter?"

Judging by his tone, Betty felt validated in leaving her translator off. "I have completed the calculations, which you can see here." With a few of her arms, she motioned at the cave wall where, in an homage to Dale and Hammy, she'd projected the formula. "Check it at your leisure, but I assure you that I have not made a mistake. I know the third letter with certainty, and I will spell it out for you with the assistance of the only known survivors of the Star Cluster B annihilation."

"There are no survivors!" shouted the halibut, who really hated Betty for some reason.

"Those are just Homo sapiens from Blerg VFP69," shouted a Lexicographer who was having an affair with the halibut and hoped this verbal support might keep that going.

Betty clapped her beak and ignored the nonsensical hollers it made as the slaves took their cue, shuffled to the center, then lowered themselves flat onto the floor. They wormed their shackled bodies the rest of the way into position, straightening out, their arms straight out above their heads.

"Behold!"

The reaction was delayed, no doubt because math was not usually presented in the form of naked Homo sapiens, but then the understanding shook the cavern.

The three bodies had taken this form:

H

"Horseshit!"

"We already discovered that letter, you cabbage!"

"Do you lack a brain in that head shell of yours? It's the same letter as before!"

Betty figured this would be the initial response.

She rolled her primary eyes. "It's not a redundancy, you void-heads. The name of the force that is everywhere and nowhere starts with HHH. Why is this so hard? You accepted HH, which *no known English word* has ever included, but suddenly, HHH is too much? Get you antennae and eye stems out of your anuses for three seconds."

"It can't be!" came another reply. "It cannot be three aitches!"

While Betty didn't know the specifics of the words being hurled her way, the guy knew incredulity when she heard it. "Sure, fiiiiine," she said. "When three *males* stand up here and tell you there's a double aitch, everyone accepts it. But when a female tells you there are three aitches and even shows her work, you suddenly can't believe it."

"A *what?*" shouted the halibut victoriously. "You're a *female?*"

The chants of *launch, launch, launch* began immediately.

Realizing her mistake, she activated her translating mechanism. "No! I didn't mean that! I don't know why I said it!"

But it was too late.

"*Launch! Launch! Launch!*"

Betty sidestepped toward the door through which the slaves had entered, but a large invertebrate guard was blocking it, and she was immediately enveloped by the jelly body, unable to escape.

Speaking of the slaves, they stayed right where they

were on the ground, but in the chaos lifted their heads enough to make eye contact. What the hell was happening? Was any of this real? One moment they were taking mushrooms at a concert in Vancouver, and the next they were here. What the hell was in those chocolates?

"Don't move," whispered one of them.

"Shouldn't the trip have ended by now?" It had been three days.

"You're just experiencing time differently," said the first, who wasn't entirely wrong. "Don't fight it. The 'shrooms are trying to show you something you need to see."

"The fuck kind of life was I living that I needed to see your balls up close?" barked the connecting line of the H.

"Maybe be a little less worried about genitals, and a little more worried about all this other shit, eh?"

"The point is *not* to worry."

Meanwhile, Betty was dragged from the auditorium, loaded into a pod, and launched on autopilot toward the nearest black hole.

And the Homo sapiens decided to embrace what the psilocybin was telling them—which was nothing because it was long out of their system—and remained on the floor, depicting the third letter in the name of God.

CHAPTER
ONE

"Duck!"

Alice Luck did as she was told and was glad she had as the glistening blade sliced through the air right where her neck had been. She shot Dan Zone a wide-eyed look of appreciation.

Stone wreckage spread out around them. Beneath their feet, crushed rock. Around them, what stone pillars remained. Above them, the clear blue sky of the planet Mo'ooz. They'd made it this far, avoided the enemy, and now safety was in sight.

Neither Alice nor Dan had stopped grinning for the last half-hour.

"There," Dan said, pointing toward a thick stone pillar farther along on the field of play. "Ample coverage."

Alice locked in on it. Definitely big enough to hide the two of them. "Ready?" she said. "Go!" She feinted like she was making a break for it, then held back, letting Dan dart out ahead of her to draw the sharp projectiles toward him. He blasted three to bits in quick succession before realizing he was without backup, his balls in the wind.

Alice cackled from her hiding spot then darted to catch up with him.

Zwarp! Zwarp!

She obliterated two blades in a row, grabbed Dan by the arm, and dragged him the rest of the way with her to cover.

As they dropped down to catch their breath, Dan shivered slightly—a symptom Alice now recognized as quantum jitters. He erupted into maniacal giggles. "Okay, you got me there. I thought you were right behind me."

They high-fived.

This was no hog wrestling, sure, but Blade Blasters was quickly becoming Alice's go-to leisure activity on their week-long vacation. The adrenaline rush of having multi-armed beings hurl blades at her so sharp they could split a hair in three was unrivaled, and while she'd put Dan's life in legitimate danger by letting him run out ahead of her, *he* had put his life in danger by playing this game in the first place. She liked that about him. The armadillo dude saw the risk in everything … and seemed to enjoy it.

The top of the stone pillar exploded in a shower of pebbles that rained down on their head.

Dan peeked out around the side of their hiding spot. "Almost to the safe zone."

"Great."

"Not great. They've lined up—all of them. They know where we are and where we need to go. It's going to rain blades down on us the second we step out from behind here."

"We have a saying back on Earth, Dan." Alice checked the charge of her blaster. It was running low, but it would be enough; she was built like a linebacker, but sprinted like a wide receiver. *"Don't bring a knife to a gun fight."* She waggled her brows at him, and he laughed.

"I like it," Dan replied. "We have one like that back on Pangoliarch. We say, 'Don't bring a slapper to a blaster bar.'"

"Feels like I'm lacking some context, but I like it. Ready?"

Dan grabbed his backup blaster from his holster. This was definitely a two-handed job.

Alice didn't leave him high and dry at the count this time. Instead, she stepped out first, cackling as the suns' light flashed off the incoming blades.

Zwarp! Zwarp!

"Woop!" she cried.

Zwarp-zwarp-zwarp! Zwarp! Zwarp-zwarp!

"Captain!"

She took her eyes off the incoming blades for a split second and realized Dan was already into the safe zone. Meanwhile, she'd stopped running.

A blade grazed her cheek, and the sting brought her back to her senses. "Balls!" She took off running. *Zwarp-zwarp!*

Dan waited in the safe zone, his arms open as he waved her on. "Almost!"

Three more blades hurled toward her. *Zzzzt.*

Her blaster was dead.

She dodged one just in time and reached for her backup. *Zzzzt.*

Oh right. That *was* her backup.

Ten yards left and no blaster to rely on. She got low.

Something nicked the heel of her Texas-flag cowboy boot, and she cursed. *Not the boots!*

She shot a scowl toward the wall of defenders on the

perimeter, but it was short-lived. The largest of the armed things was winding up. The curved blade flew, slicing through the air at an angle that made it impossible to judge how severely it would arc.

Zwarp!

It fell from the air, nothing but molten metal now, as Alice made a final leap into the safe zone.

And Dan, who'd left safety to blast away the final threat, followed right on her heels.

She flopped onto her back, panting on the cool green grass at the edge of the playing field, and stared up at the bright blue sky. With each heave of her chest, she let the adrenaline pulse through her veins. The comedown would follow shortly, but for now, she felt indestructible.

Ah, there it was, the dull ache in her arm where a blaster had scorched it on Britannica. Allura's special cream had worked magic to help it rapidly heal in the last few days, but the heavy use of it on the course was clearly more than a doctor would recommend.

A pearlescent, plated hand appeared in her field of vision, blocking out one of the suns. She grabbed it and let Dan pull her up to her feet.

"Great round, Captain."

"You saved my ass there, Dan. Drinks on me."

"Sounds— Wait, you're bleeding."

Alice brought a hand up to her face, touching her cheek. When she pulled away, her fingertips were red. "Eh, not too bad." Compared to the blaster she'd taken to the arm on the previous mission, this was nothing. The goop Allura had given her for a speedy recovery worked like a charm, anyway. All that was left less than a week later was a small bit of scarring, hardly more than some texture where her skin had been singed off.

She poked at her cheek near the wound. "I can hardly feel it."

"That'll change once the adrenaline wears off."

"Then we better get sloshed before that happens." She patted him on the shoulder, but her mirth died when she realized her hand had grazed metal. "What the…" She stepped to the side to get a look at his back. "Christ on a cracker, Dan." One of the blades jutted from his back. "You're hit."

"Huh?" He groped around until he found it. "Oh. Heh. Didn't even notice." He cringed. "Oh void, did it rip my shirt badly?" The blade had lodged itself in Nick Carter's head as he posed with the rest of the Backstreet Boys above a list of tour dates from 1999.

Alice examined it. "Not badly. Poor Nick has seen better days. Maybe not *much* better."

"Nick? Not Kevin?"

"No, Kevin is fine."

Dan found the handle of the blade, and with a grunt pulled it from his armored back, tossing it aside.

In a lot of ways, having a minister of weapons and culture on her crew was hugely reassuring. He could tell her all the faux pas to avoid when they met new species or visited strange planets. He'd undoubtedly saved her ass that way many times already. But she often forgot that he was obsessed with the culture of Blerg VFP69, known to her as Earth or home, and when he dropped strange nuggets like his favorite Backstreet Boy, it made her head hurt a little.

Besides … Kevin?

She'd always been an AJ girl.

"You're all right?" she asked, eyeing the small tear in his T-shirt for any signs of blood. But it was dry enough.

"Of course! I'm fine. Why look like this if the armor doesn't do anything?" He held out his arms demonstratively, and the sunlight danced off the pearly plates poking out of the sleeves of his shirt.

"You're making me feel naked and exposed," she said, then nodded toward the lodge—specifically, in her mind, toward the bar.

A few minutes later, as the bartender, whom Alice could only describe as "squiggly," took their order, Dan said, "We should probably grab something for Vel while we're here."

"Good call."

And though they ordered a drink for her, Alice suspected the lieutenant wouldn't need it. Vel had taken an immediate liking to one of the beach waiters, and Alice was pretty sure the warrior woman hadn't moved from her shady chair since they'd arrived at the resort five days earlier.

Sure enough, they found Lieutenant Machiavelli right where they'd left her that morning.

"Susy," Alice said, stepping in front of one of the suns and causing Vel to crack open an eye. "Have you even gotten up to go to the bathroom?" She set the cold tropical drink on the small table, next to the fresh one already there.

"Why don't you let me worry about that, Captain?"

"I would, but you don't seem to be capable of worrying about *anything* this week."

Vel shut her eye again. "You say that like it's a bad thing. Isn't the whole reason the Depot gives us a week off between missions to help us relax and *stop* worrying?"

Alice stuck a fist on her hip. "Technically, yes. But that doesn't mean I thought you could do it."

"What are you saying, Captain? You think I'm overly serious?"

"Yes, that's exactly what I'm saying. And I like that about you, Susy. I need someone to keep us on track, otherwise, it falls to me."

"I would hate to leave some responsibility for you … *Captain*."

Alice grunted. "I see the point you're trying to make. Still, *why* are you so relaxed?"

Dan added, "That's what I've been wondering, too. No judgment, just curiosity. Is this how you work through trauma?"

"Trauma? What trauma?" Keeping her eyes closed, Vel reached over and grabbed her drink from the table, slowly and leisurely taking a long sip before setting it back down.

Alice looked around for any possible ghasselite formations but found none. "Were you not on that last mission with us? Did I *hallucinate* your being there when Liz Windsor announced that the Depot had eliminated all life within an entire star cluster because we refused to match the Yoken?"

"I was there."

"Then you know that we're the bad guys."

Though Alice considered it to be the obvious conclusion from the given data points, no one had previously said it aloud, and now that she had, she expected a much stronger reaction than what she was getting from her second-in-command.

Vel shrugged. "Eh, if you want to believe that, sure."

"Of course I don't *want* to believe it," Alice snapped, wondering how they'd ended up on such a buzzkill of a topic when they *should've* been soothing the adrenaline crash with copious alien alcohols.

"Then don't believe it," Vel said plainly. "You're so great at escaping reality, I'm not sure why you'd stop now that reality is this ugly."

"Because … because … someone has to face it!"

Vel chuckled. "Is that what you're doing? Playing Blade Blasters as a way of facing reality? You got a little something, by the way." She gestured at her own cheek, and Alice hurriedly wiped away the blood from the cut, smudging it more than clearing it.

"For the record," Vel continued, "the reason I can relax is because I know what I'm up against now. I understand how this game works. That's all I need to know. Now I can win it."

"Game?" Alice said. "What game?"

"The game we're all trapped in. The one we keep playing." Then, "No, not Blade Blasters. Working for the Depot."

"Please, then, Susy. Explain to me how it works."

Vel took another sip. "No point. You wouldn't listen long enough."

Alice snapped her head toward her lieutenant. "Sorry, what? Crazy bird thing landed in that tree. Go on."

Dan chugged the rest of his drink.

"The Depot is a tyrant," Vel explained. "They will murder large swaths of the universe under the pretense of keeping the peace, but it's really for power. And now I know that as long as we go along with them and occasionally throw them a planet to wipe out, they probably won't kill us. That's how we win."

Alice and Dan shared a bummed look.

"You're okay with that?" Dan asked.

"Of course not. But surviving, given the circumstances, is what I call success. So I'm okay with it. And I'm okay with reading this book on the beach between missions." She held up a copy of *Sucked by the Black Hole*.

Alice read the title. "What … is that?"

"I don't know. Allura recommended it, and you know what? I'm enjoying it. I'm enjoying sitting on this beach, getting drunk in the sun, and reading the dirtiest book I've ever laid eyes on. Do you know how many things I've genuinely enjoyed in my life? Two. This"—she waved the book around, keeping her place in it with her thumb—"and killing my evil twin."

"The fuck?"

Vel waved her off. "It's a long story, but it had to be done. Now, did you need something else from me, or can I get back to reading?"

"Do you know where Caid is?"

Vel pointed out toward the waves.

"Geez, he's still out there?" Alice turned to Dan. "We'd better go check on him."

"I'll meet you out there. I need another." He held up his empty glass.

Alice chugged the rest of hers. "I'll take another, too."

As Dan headed back to the bar, Alice kicked off her boots and shuffled across the sand to the water's edge. As the sea of this strange planet licked at her toes, she shielded her eyes and located the crew's therapist floating on his multicolored holographic raft.

The water didn't get deeper than her waist for a mile out from shore, and though it was crystal clear, she proceeded cautiously. She'd spent too many summers on the Texas Gulf Coast and been stung by a jellyfish twice. Those creepy little invertebrates were upsetting enough; she didn't want to think about what shit might exist in the water on a foreign planet.

She called out to him.

He didn't respond.

She called out again, louder this time.

Still no response.

The organic hologram merely continued to sit cross-legged on his raft, staring out into the aqua expanse. He'd been meditating like this for most of the trip, only occasionally checking in on shore to see how everyone was feeling. He seemed uncharacteristically relieved every time they blew him off and he was able to return to this raft in the ocean.

How could someone so ancient be so goddamn sensitive, she wondered.

There was no doubt that he'd been hit the hardest by the unlucky fate of those in Star Cluster B. The whole mission had been upsetting for him, from dealing with Aubert Orleans's moodiness to discovering the bodies of his old crew members in that cave to …

The mass slaughter.

The mass slaughter justified by her decision to terminate the matchmaking mission.

The eugenics mission.

Something sharp and mean stirred inside her brain. A thought. Not a good one.

She blinked it away and realized her eyes were wet in the corners. "Ew." She wiped away the moisture, then put her back to the sea. "Dan!" She waved to get his attention, then hurried over to get started on the next drink.

CHAPTER
TWO

Alice watched from her captain's chair on the bridge of *Emergence* as they broke through the Earth's atmosphere and made for Paper Depot, Austin, Texas, U.S.A.—also known as the Depot's universal headquarters.

Before she'd ever known about anything of this—back when she was still applying for jobs and hoping her perfectly fine boyfriend of five years didn't get a bug up his ass about proposing—she'd driven past the Paper Depot plenty of times, assuming (silly her) that it was simply an office supply store.

It was that. But it was also so much more.

Emergence stayed hidden in a cloud as the hangar door opened in the back alley behind the store, and once they finally lowered, Alice got a glimpse of the street below. She recognized almost none of it. What was once a coffee shop now appeared to be some sort of greenhouse. What was once a legendary dance hall now appeared to be ... nothing. Just a dilapidated pile of rubble with plants already blooming from it. Probably a condo soon enough.

That was life in Austin. Businesses came and went,

restaurants especially. She'd been to Austin a few times for rodeos when she was younger, and almost nothing that had existed then was still around by the time she moved there after college. It was a city of progress, of failing fast, of trends and innovation.

But still, why was it so overgrown? Had there been so much overgrowth the last time she'd seen the area? Had the real estate bubble finally burst in a big way? Or maybe it was that virus Liz Windsor had mentioned, followed by an earthquake. No, surely not. The closest fault line was supposed to be long dormant.

The rest of the crew of DeepService Team One had opted to stay in their rooms for the trip back from vacation, and Alice was strangely glad for the peace. She wasn't completely alone, anyway. Allura 4000 was always there.

"Ohh, it feels nice to slip inside again," said the operating system as the door to the Depot hangar shut behind them. *Emergence* touched down with the slightest of jolts.

The rest of the crew joined Alice silently on the bridge, and they took the elevator down to the lower deck together.

Liz Windsor was already waiting on the other side of the ship's port as it opened, her huge grin greeting the group like an unwelcome foghorn. "Look at you! So well rested, I can tell. Captain Luck, your tan is incredible! And Minister Zone, I've never seen your armor so reflective!"

Dan found himself blushing at the compliment, despite his trepidation about being back in Depot territory. If they knew all the things he was starting to suspect about them …

Liz Windsor gasped. "Lieutenant Machiavelli. I—I've never seen you so *relaxed*. You're absolutely radiant!"

Vel, who normally had her dark hair pulled back in a tight ponytail or braid, had opted to let it down on vacation. She didn't see why she should worry about looking like a mercenary now anyway. That wasn't necessary for the game they were playing, and, in fact, looking more feminine and less, well, scary as hell might even work in her favor. So she let her long raven hair hang down past her shoulders.

"Thanks," she said, casually accepting the compliment.

"I know, isn't she hot?" Alice said resentfully. She still wasn't pleased with Vel's new attitude. Someone had to take this seriously, and if it wasn't Vel, then it probably fell to her.

It certainly hadn't fallen to Caid, who looked as peaceful as Alice had ever seen him. Whatever he did out on that floaty must've worked. Damn. She glanced at Dan and was relieved that he, at least, didn't look relaxed.

Then again, his shoulders were always a little stiff—it came with having plated armor.

"Doug has already brewed the coffee, and it's waiting for you in the lounge."

"Do you have any herbal tea?" Caid asked. "I've been off caffeine."

And instead of pointing out that *of course* he was off caffeine, due to not having mass that could hold the molecules of caffeine within him, Liz Windsor simply said, "Oh, that's wonderful! Yes, of course we can find something for you." She tip-tapped across the hangar and held open the door for them to enter the hallway of the underground headquarters. "This is why we do the week's vacation in between missions. It does absolute wonders for the health of the crew."

Without realizing it, Alice touched the cut on her cheek, which was healing, thanks to Allura's magical goop, but still had a ways to go. "Yeah, very healthy," she muttered.

Caid caught up to Vel as they walked down the hall. "I meant to say it earlier, but you do look radiant. I'm impressed with how you took advantage of the vacation."

She eyed him. "Thanks. Looks like you've healed your trauma."

Caid pressed his palms together and bowed his head slightly. "Not all of it, but enough to keep going. I had breakthroughs out on the water. I kept wishing you would join me, but I see now that you had your own way of recovering, and I'm glad you let your body take the lead. It always knows what it needs."

"Not body," Vel replied. "Mind."

"And heart, I hope?"

"What heart?" She strolled past Liz Windsor, who held open the door, and entered the lounge.

Once they were seated around the leather couches with their coffee—Caid with his holographic hibiscus mint tea—Liz Windsor folded her hands in her lap and seemed to reset with a curt exhale followed by a fresh smile. "I believe we left on unfortunate terms, and I would like to clear the air. What happened to Star Cluster B was not your fault. Nor was it the Depot's. As I'm sure Caid will agree, someone else's harmful behavior is not your fault. By responding with strict boundaries, you are not harming that person in return, though they may act as if you are. You are simply protecting yourself, and I believe we are all entitled to protect not only ourselves but the innocent lives around us."

"You mean like the containment field around Star Cluster B was already doing?" Alice asked.

Liz Windsor blinked three times in rapid succession then replied, "The situation had changed. I'm not entirely sure that I'm allowed to tell you this, but I will because I know it will change your mind about things. The Depot had reliable intelligence saying that a terrorist group had developed the technology to break down the containment field and allow the nastier elements of an already nasty cluster to escape into the rest of the universe. Our hope was that we could send DeepService Team One to one of the more civilized planets on record there to extract some good from the cluster, a little hope that could spread a warning about what happens when a cluster falls to greed."

"Falls to greed?" Dan asked, staring through narrowed almond eyes at the liaison. "I don't remember hearing anything about that."

Liz Windsor met his gaze, and there was something sharp in her expression. "What did you think led to the Depot instituting the containment field, Minister Zone?"

"Oh, I, uh. I don't know. I haven't heard anything about that."

"Then is it so hard to believe greed was the cause?"

"No, I suppose not."

But whose greed? he thought.

"The Depot wanted to rescue anyone they could from the cluster, I promise you that. It's always been the Depot's mission to save as much life as possible in our universe, both sentient and not. That's what their Red Initiative is all about, for instance."

"Their *what?*" Alice asked.

"Their— Oh, right. It's like what you might know on Earth as a 'green initiative.' There's a galaxy where all the organic plant life is red. Reckless behavior by the superior sentient beings was causing the various ecosystems to fail, so the Depot stepped in to protect the environment."

That was much less gory than Alice had—

"Yes, it required a bit of a drawn-out campaign of slaughtering the superior sentient beings on those planets, but in the end, the ecosystem was spared. In fact, it *loved* all the fresh compost and has been flourishing ever since. Many hot vacation spots there now. With strict environmental guidelines, of course."

"Ah," Alice said, remembering the overgrowth in the streets around Paper Depot.

"The message I wish to convey to you all," Liz Windsor continued, "is that the Depot didn't act solely on your report of the Yoken people and their likelihood of redemption. Plans were already in place, and we were simply looking for any bit of hope we could find that Star Cluster B was not as bad off as we'd suspected. The Depot is *optimistic* about life, if nothing else. It can be hard for those to whom I report to admit that some groups are simply not worth saving, and that the humane-but-necessary action is to eliminate them for the safety of the rest."

"Couldn't they have shored up the containment field instead?" Dan asked. "Made certain that no one could tunnel out of it?"

Liz Windsor's smile tightened. "Perhaps they could have played that game, but at what cost? The amount of planetary taxes going toward the maintenance of that field was astronomical, no pun intended. It's really not fair to the planetary governments and the people within them to keep paying every year for people like the Yoken to live and breathe."

Alice's legs wouldn't stop twitching. They did that sometimes when a situation got ugly like this. She tried to relegate the manic energy to her toes, making them wiggle undetected in her boots. "Whatever happened to preserving the ecosystems?" she asked. "You said the Depot eliminated all life in the cluster. I assume that means everything. The trees, the bugs, those little walking shrubs."

Liz Windsor tilted her head to the side like a patient kindergarten teacher. "Yes, but where *Emergence* landed on Trauna was almost entirely demonstrative of what that planet and others in the cluster had become. The people living there had stripped it of all it was worth. Famine was often a way of life. Nothing, and I mean *nothing* was healthy—or could ever be again."

Alice was about to protest, remembering the banquet hall in the palace, but then she remembered the food they'd been served in the cave by the three wives. That was probably more representative anyway. "Even still, doesn't it seem extreme? Why does the Depot get to make that decision in the first place?"

"Someone has to," the liaison replied. "You understand that it's not a simple or easy call by any means. No one wants to have to make it. That's why so many planets are happy to leave those responsibilities up to the wisdom and judgment of the Depot. Prior to the Depot's presence in our universe, no other governing group possessed the necessary wisdom or ability to create peace. But the Depot did. It's the reason we can sit here on Blerg VFP69 right now and enjoy a hot beverage without fearing that a band of slobbering renegades will burst in and hack us to bits, but only after raping any of us with physical matter and a hole to stick something in. So yes, execution is not pretty, but it's necessary. I believe your state government feels the same, does it not?"

Alice shifted on the leather cushion. "Yeah, well, you got me there."

"The universe is a vast place," Liz Windsor concluded. "You can fixate on all the living beings in Star Cluster B who were eliminated—quickly and painlessly, I might add —or you can remember how many uncountable beings within the universe were spared what might happen if those from Cluster B ever escaped."

Because Vel didn't appear at all unsettled about this, Alice decided not to worry. "That's one way to look at—"

The door to the lounge shot open, banging against the wall, and a man in *lederhosen* marched in, yodeling so loudly and passionately it sounded like he was trying to summon the spirits of ancient yodelers past.

"The fuck?" Alice jumped to her feet instantly, but Vel still beat her to it. Clearly, this *wasn't* an expected part of "the game."

"Is he armed?" Vel asked, drawing a weapon no one realized she had on her.

"Yoo-dle-owdle-ay-ee-oo!"

"Is there a bomb on him?" Dan shouted.

The yodeler continued marching toward them, singing his … battle cry? None could be sure because no one knew what the hell was happening.

"Shoot him, Susy!"

"Is that an order, Captain?"

"Yes! I order you to—"

A thick, smoking hole appeared in the middle of the

yodeler's *lederhosen,* and he fell to the ground. The yodeling had stopped, and in its place was gurgling.

Caid clutched at his face as they stared at the dead man on the floor. "Liz Windsor," he whispered. "Who …?"

The liaison blinked down at the body. "I haven't the foggiest."

And the strangest part of this situation was that it *was* the likeliest of all possibilities on a quantum scale.

But it didn't happen in the reality we're following, only in most of those we're not following.

In ours, Alice said, "That's one way to look at it, I reckon."

Dan began shaking and jerking uncontrollably on the couch cushion next to her, overtaken by the quantum jitters. She jumped to her feet, not because of a yodeler, but to make room for Dan. Vel sprang into action, too, but again, not for a yodeler. The lieutenant grabbed the top half of Dan's shaking body while the captain grabbed his ankles and the two of them helped him lie flat on the couch until this round of jitters subsided.

"Oh dear," Liz Windsor muttered. "Oh my, this is not good."

But the fit slowed before long, and once Alice felt sure he wouldn't twitch his way onto the hard floor, she let go of his legs and took a step back. "That's strange."

"Sure is," said Vel. "Usually we've narrowly escaped danger when his jitters start."

"But we were just sitting here talking," Alice added. "Nothing seemed unlikely. What did we miss?" She looked to Caid and Liz Windsor for answers, but both of them shook their heads, equally clueless.

From the couch, Dan groaned. "What happened?" He tried to sit up, but Vel pushed him back down to rest.

"Besides your quantum jitters?" she replied. "Nothing, as far as we know. Has that happened before, where you can't figure out why you had them?"

Dan shut his eyes and exhaled. "I can usually tell."

"That's right," Alice said. "You got them when I blasted that asteroid through the cosmic gate, and then when the Alliance shot at you on Bacc'nalia, then again—"

"All in obvious situations," Dan replied.

"Very interesting," said Liz Windsor. "I encourage you to explore this more, but if Minister Zone is recovering all right, we do have other business to attend to, as I'm sure you understand."

"Other business?" Alice asked.

"Yes! Your next client. She's waiting in one of the conference rooms for us, ready to be introduced."

"Right," Alice muttered. "Client. We have jobs." The concept of employment was still strange to her, as was that of being an adult who needed employment.

Although, technically, she had enough money now to quit and retire wherever she wanted in the universe.

She was thinking South Padre Island. Maybe she could make Blade Blasters a thing there.

"Help yourself to another coffee refill if you'd like, then please follow me. I think you're going to love her. You especially, Lieutenant Machiavelli."

And nobody, not even Vel, liked the sound of that.

"Right in here," Liz Windsor said, holding open the door to the conference room.

As soon as Alice stepped inside, leading the crew, she planted her boots and gaped.

This day was getting stranger and stranger. First, the jitters out of nowhere, and now this? "Susy?" Alice muttered from the corner of her mouth. "I thought you said you killed her."

Alice was blocking the way, but Vel shoved her to the side enough to enter. And then she, too, stopped in her tracks. Instinctively, her hand reached for the blaster that nobody in this reality knew she had on her. "Ace? How are you—?"

The women stared at each other, and Vel's duplicate looked as shocked to see Vel as Vel looked to see her.

Alice knew that if Vel had worn her hair up in her usual ponytail, they would be in dangerous *Parent Trap* territory, but thankfully, her lieutenant had opted for the more relaxed look.

"Is that not your twin?" Alice asked.

"It can't be. I don't have a twin," Vel muttered, "not anymore." She glared at the woman, her blaster finger itching. "Ace?"

The duplicate spoke. "Is that what you think my name is? Ace? It's not."

Liz Windsor squeezed between the captain and lieutenant, then paused. "Oh! Oh my! Yes, yes, I thought she looked familiar, but I'm only now realizing why." The liaison laughed and then proceeded toward the client at the far end of the conference table. "Very much an uncanny resemblance, huh?"

Uncanny didn't describe it. It was *identical*.

"Come, come," Liz Windsor said, waving them all in. "There's plenty of room for two fearless warrior women!" She giggled, but no one else appeared ready to relax.

"The fuck is going on?" Dan breathed in Alice's ear, and instead of bothering to respond, which she didn't have a clue how to do anyway, she enjoyed that the minister of weapons and culture had adopted one of her favorite words. For better or worse, she was rubbing off on him.

The carbon copy at the end of the table stood, waiting at attention, her jaw visibly clenched. Liz Windsor did everyone the honors. "This is our new client, Captain Quark Leviathan. Captain Leviathan, this is Captain Alice Luck, Lieutenant Susy Machiavelli, Minister Dan Zone, and our crew aid, Caid Sonorian."

Vel had never been so confused in her life. She'd watched her evil twin die. This couldn't be Ace. And yet this woman standing before them looked more like Vel than an identical twin might. Had there been a third? A triplet who escaped? It was all too unlikely.

She glared at Captain Leviathan, looking for an

imperfection, but all she could see was a scar that crept down from her hairline, disappeared into the eyebrow, then reappeared on the cheek. Ugh. It was so badass. Vel had never coveted an injury before, but all kinds of strange things were happening now.

And while the appearance of her doppelgänger stole some of her certainty that she knew what game they were playing, it certainly kept things interesting.

Unclenching her own jaw, but not letting her guard down, Vel bowed her head and said, "Captain Leviathan, it's a pleasure to meet you. We're honored to have you as a client."

Upon direct communication between the two women, the elephant in the room grew into a Barbatooniq, which is a creature that only exists on the planet Pou and looks startlingly like an elephant, but is twenty times larger (and exhales noxious gas).

"Please," replied the client, "call me Lev."

The pleasantries had turned into a battle.

"Of course, Lev. Call me …" She didn't want to say it. This was too weird. But she had to. "Call me Vel."

Alice gasped. "Wait! Lev? Vel? Are you kidding? Your names are mirror images!" She chuckled. "Man, this is *so* weird, isn't it? What are the odds?"

"Yeah," Dan said, "what *are* they?"

"The universe is a delightfully surprising place, is it not?" Liz Windsor asked rhetorically. Then, motioning around the table, "Sit, sit! No point standing around when we have these delightfully ergonomic chairs."

Once they were seated, Vel picking the chair opposite the client at the head of the table, Liz Windsor continued the introductions. "Captain Leviathan has come all the way from a parallel universe, much like our own

Lieutenant Machiavelli, but has settled down with the people of the planet Del'evvia and become a beloved diplomat on their behalf."

Alice took in the woman's attire. It was almost identical to the sleek leather armor Vel had worn the first day the crew met. Lev's were all shades of rich green, though, where Vel's had been the expected browns. "That's what diplomats wear on Del'evvia?"

Captain Leviathan smiled, and it was disarmingly lovely. "Not usually, but old habits die hard, as they say, and I wasn't always a diplomat."

"Not even close to it!" Liz Windsor proclaimed proudly. "The biography you provided was absolutely fascinating reading, frankly. Voted Best Savior of the Downtrodden five years in a row, awarded the Depot's Intergalactic Medal of Justified Murder not once, but *twice*, and a *four*-time recipient of the Crab Nebula's highest honor of Bloodthirsty Renegade."

"Oh, nice!" Alice said. "Susy won that a bunch of times, too. How many was it? Five?"

Vel responded through gritted teeth, "Three."

"Ah, well, there's still time," Alice said, patting her second-in-command on the shoulder.

"Best Savior of the Downtrodden is no small accomplishment," Dan said. "I've never met someone who earned that award. What did you do to receive it?"

Captain Leviathan blushed and waved him off. "It was years ago. And the whole award thing is a little embarrassing, isn't it? You do the right thing because it's the right thing to do, not because someone will give you a medal for it. Honestly"—she leaned toward him, and instinctively, he moved closer to her—"I had to be dragged kicking and screaming to the ceremony. Those things bore me to tears. A bunch of sentient beings patting themselves on the back."

Alice leaned toward Vel. "I like her already."

"You liked Aubert Orleans when you first met him, too," Vel snapped.

Dan said, "And now you're a diplomat. Wow. I bet that's even more dangerous at times."

Captain Leviathan shrugged casually. "Occasionally, but I couldn't justify being a fighter my whole life. I decided I'd done enough fighting. It was tempting to move on and do something quiet, or maybe work in the private sector for someone like the Depot, but ultimately, I felt like I needed to actively balance the scales, not retreat and withdraw."

"That's very admirable of you," Caid said.

Vel snapped her head toward him. *You too?* she thought. But before she could worry about that further, he added, "I believe Vel has also pursued that path. Instead of tearing families apart, she's now working to build them, to bring groups of people together to promote tranquility and love."

"Maybe *love* is a strong word," said Vel, with a hint of false modesty.

"I don't know that I'm here on a mission of *love*," Captain Leviathan said, "so much as reproduction. I think we all know the two things aren't always the same." She grinned, and the rest of the table couldn't help but return the smile.

Except Vel. She could help it.

That bitch had taken her quip, repeated it in *more* words, and earned approval for it?

Vel was losing. She was losing this game.

I'd do anything for a yodeler to pop in here and disrupt this, she thought. Then, *A yodeler? Why the hell did I think of a yodeler?*

"Speaking of which," Alice said, "what's up with your planet's birth rate? Tell us about that."

"My pleasure, Captain Luck."

"Alice, please."

"As long as you call me Lev." Captain Leviathan beamed. "The people of Del'evvia are mostly happy. I represent the Fnori people, who are undeniably the dominant species there. They look nothing like me, as I'm simply an immigrant they've adopted as their own. Theirs was one of the few planets that avoided involvement in the Great War, and harmony has always been a guiding principle of theirs. But in the last twenty years, the reproduction rate has plummeted to nearly nothing. With an aging population, we're facing a crisis of having enough caretakers for the elderly. But there are plenty of other pressing issues surrounding this. The children born in the last decade suffer grave illness and a pugnacious attitude from birth. No one knows why they're so ornery, but it's wrecking the peace of the planet."

"From birth? You think it might be a birth defect?" Alice asked.

"Possibly. We don't know what it is. But I've heard so much about DeepService Team One that I recommended we solicit your help, and the Guiding Elders agreed. It's well known that DeepService Team One has a one hundred percent success rate in matches."

Alice cringed as Vel gripped her knee beneath the table before the captain could say something stupid to the contrary.

"Yes," Alice said, sounding slightly constipated, "never failed."

"I have full faith," said Liz Windsor, "that this crew is exactly who you need to assess the problem and match the Fnori people with another compatible race, if the situation calls for it. They are all *excellent* at what they do." She addressed the others. "As you might've guessed, Captain Leviathan has requested that she join you on the mission. I believe she offers invaluable skills of diplomacy and insight into those you'll be working with. Not that you don't *also* offer those things, Minister Zone. In fact, the two of you are so good at what you do that I can't wait to see how you work together! Magic, I'm sure!"

"No insult taken, Liz Windsor," Dan replied. "I'm excited to have Captain Leviathan's help. A former warrior like her will undoubtedly enjoy a tour of the onboard weaponry."

The client held up a hand. "That's very kind of you, and I understand why you would assume that, but I don't handle weapons anymore. I gave that up when I dedicated my life to peace."

Dan narrowed his eyes at her. "But weapons ... weapons are necessary to keep the peace."

"Only if you're overly attached to living," she replied, not unkindly.

Dan and Alice shared a quick glance. They were both very attached to living.

"This extra person does mean that upgrading to a larger ship would be—"

"Not happening," Alice said. "We need *Emergence* and we need Allura."

"Very well," Liz Windsor said, her cheery façade faltering in the slightest way. "Dan, would you be okay rooming with Cald again?"

Before he could answer, Vel piped in. "I'll stay with Captain Luck. Lev can have my room."

"Oh," said Liz Windsor. "All right, then. If you're fine with that, Captain Luck?"

"Hell yeah!" Alice offered a hand, and Vel slapped it reluctantly. "Sleepover!"

After a bit more housekeeping by the liaison, Liz Windsor adjourned the meeting and instructed the crew to load up.

On the way out of the conference room, Caid caught up to Vel, leaned over, and whispered, "Identity is a wild beast. I get it. I'll make time for you right away."

CHAPTER
FOUR

Alice scrubbed the towel over her wet hair as she left the small bathroom of her captain's chambers. "Pretty sure I'm gonna be cleaning sand from my crack for another month."

Vel looked up from her small bed in the corner, where she'd been researching Captain Quark Leviathan's background. So far, it all checked out. Not an evil twin, as far as Vel could see. At least, not hers. "Maybe I should've roomed with Dan."

Alice tossed the wet towel onto the foot of her own small bed. "You're really going to tell me you spent all that time on the beach, and you didn't get sand in your ass crack?"

"I'm not going to tell you anything about my ass crack, Captain. That's the point."

"Please stop calling me captain. You make it sound like an insult. Alice. Or, if you want to act like the boys in my high school geography class, Easy A."

Vel arched a brow at Alice. "You were an A student?"

"Uh, no. I don't think that's why— Never mind. Call me Alice. We're roomies now, after all!"

"I haven't forgotten it."

Alice remained in her soft bathrobe and flopped back onto her bed, staring at Vel across the room. "What happened to the relaxed woman with a boozy drink in one hand and weird alien smut in the other?"

Vel sat up. "What *happened*? A parallel version of me showed up."

"Is that what she is? A parallel version of you?"

"Yes. She's not my twin. I watched that bitch die. Lev is clearly me from a parallel universe."

"Or you're her from a parallel universe."

Vel grunted.

"Does this mean the game has changed? Is that why you're not relaxed? Or did you run out or relaxation? Probably both, right?"

Vel set the research tablet on the mattress next to her. "I have a weird feeling, is all. I still understand the Depot's overarching game, but I don't understand why they brought Lev on as a client. It's my understanding that they have thousands of applicants weekly. Why choose her? It feels personal."

"Taking on a parallel version of one of the crew as a client? Yeah, I'd say that's about as personal as it gets." Alice paused, and her eyes grew large. "Shit. You don't think we'll run into a copy of me, do you?"

"I certainly hope not."

"Supposing—from a mathematical perspective, obviously—supposing I met a parallel version of me, and we, I dunno, made out. Would that screw with the fabric of space?"

Before Vel could muster the energy to answer, someone spoke outside their door.

"Alice! Vel! Hey, can I speak with you?"

They looked at one another. "Is that Caid?" Alice asked.

"Sounds like him, and anyone else would knock."

When Alice opened the door and saw who was there, she jumped back, clutching at her robe to keep from accidentally exposing herself. "Who the fuck?"

As Vel got a peek, her hand shot immediately to the blaster under her pillow.

"Relax," said the man at the door. "It's me. It's me."

To be sure, Alice took a swing at him. Her hand went straight through. It really was Caid. "Why do you look like that?"

"Never mind," Vel said, pushing her aside. "Get in here before Lev sees you." She shut the door behind Caid who did not look at all like Caid.

"You can change your appearance," Vel said, drawing the obvious conclusion from the man standing in front of her.

"Sometimes, but not like this. I evolve with the expansion of the universe and the dominant life forms within it, though I don't usually change in an instant. But that's what happened. I didn't even feel it. When I parted ways with you on the bridge I looked like my old self, didn't I?"

The women confirmed.

"Then at some point, I changed. I caught sight of myself in the reflecting pool in my room, and wowee! I gave myself a fright!"

Though Caid looked completely different from his usual hot-surfer-dude-with-a-guitar self, his new form was still strangely familiar to Alice, and not at all unappealing. But where did she recognize him from?

"Oh shit." She gaped at him as it clicked.

Caid had never looked so startled. "What is it? Did I change again?" He held his arms out in front of him.

"No! I know who you are!"

"He's Caid," Vel said. "I thought you understood that."

"I mean I know who he looks like."

"I look like someone?"

"*Exactly* like him."

"Who?" said Caid and Vel.

"I dated this guy in college who was a filmmaker. Well, he called himself that, but mostly he filmed girls in the Quad without them knowing and then stitched it together and added My Chemical Romance songs in the background. Doesn't matter. The point is that he made me watch all these old movies with him before he was in the mood to bone. And by bone, I mean him lie there like a drowned rat. Again, doesn't matter. The point is that you look like the actor Cary Grant."

"Why would Caid look like the actor Cary Grant?"

Alice blew a long raspberry. "Beats the hell outta me. But he does. Look." She grabbed her own tablet and brought up pictures.

The other two were speechless.

Vel said, "It's so—"

"Random," Alice finished correctly. "It's random as hell. But at least he's still smokin' hot, right?"

Vel looked at Caid, but not in a sexy way. "What affects an organic hologram?" she asked.

Caid threw his arms up. "Nothing! Not physically, at least. Emotionally, a lot affects me, and I won't be shamed for that. But physically? Nothing should alter my appearance except the slow march of universal evolution."

"Doesn't evolution jump forward sometimes?" Alice asked. "One weird gene mutation takes over? Maybe all life forms are slowly evolving toward a single point of looking like Cary Grant."

Her theory, though well meaning, did nothing to calm Caid's nerves.

"I feel so powerless," he said. "And I know that I am technically powerless as a non-physical being, but there's also so much I can do to influence others using my heart and mind. But this? I've never felt so out of control."

Vel had seen Caid cry before, so that wasn't what alarmed her. What alarmed her was that he was right, that he was powerless in this when by all accounts he shouldn't be, that yet another strange and unlikely thing was happening. It set her nerves on edge.

"Shh," Alice said, patting at the air around his shoulder. "It's okay. This is weird, sure, but you're still hot. It could be much worse. Don't worry, everything will be okay."

But while the captain might believe that, Vel had serious doubts. Nothing was trending toward *okay*.

CHAPTER
FIVE

Caid was back to his normal appearance by the time they met again on the bridge an hour later. Alice was glad for it, not only because it made his odds of crying far lower, but because she didn't want to explain it to the client. No way Dan would react calmly to it, either.

It went unspoken that no one would bring it up now that they were in the group, so instead, they pretended it hadn't happened.

Alice was especially talented at that.

She put it out of her mind, settled in her captain's chair, and allowed Captain Leviathan to lead the conversation.

Because the client remained standing, so did Vel, her arms crossed over her chest, posting herself near but not in her lieutenant's chair. Dan was lounging in the gunner's seat by the manual weapon controls, and Caid observed the conversation from a distance, strumming his holographic guitar lazily to produce a soft and soothing soundtrack.

"I figured I should do my research ahead of time before

joining an esteemed team such as this," Lev was explaining.

Alice stopped daydreaming about blade blasting and tuned in. Absent-mindedly, she ran a finger over the cut on her face. "If you know the specific names, Allura can pull them up for us."

"The first are the Hamatachi people of Swort VFP381."

"Allura?"

"Yes, father?"

Alice jerked her chin back. "Whoa. Um, Allura, are you okay? That's *not* what we agreed on."

"You don't wish for me to call you that?" the operating system's voice replied as if nothing extra creepy had happened.

"One hundred percent no. Sounds like you're about to give me your confession. Anyway, can you pull up information on the Hamatachis of Swort VFP381?"

"Yes, padre."

"No, no, no." Alice waved her hands in front of her. "Please no. That's the same."

Alice looked to Dan for an answer. He shrugged, merely fascinated by the large connotative differences of each name. Earth culture was wild.

The front window of *Emergence* activated its semi-opaque screen function, and up popped six upright figures, each of them naked and humanoid except for the single pogo stick of a leg they had.

Alice wasn't into lime-green skin herself, but thankfully she wasn't the one seeking a mate. The job of DeepService Team One was simple in theory: match apex species with apex species from other planets. Alien husbandry.

In practice, the job was not so simple, if the crew's first two missions were any indication.

Alice stared at the naked rotating figures on the screen and frowned as she tried to imagine banging one of them. Nah, definitely not her type. Not even on a dare.

Okay, maybe a double-dog dare.

However, Quark Leviathan had chosen this as a possibility for the Fnori people, then they were probably *aesthetically* suitable.

"Why are there six of them?" Alice asked. "There's usually only three. Male, female, intersex."

"As you can see if we zoom in, there are two kinds of males, two kinds of females, and two kinds of demales within this species."

"Demales?" Alice asked incredulously.

"Yes."

"What are those?"

Captain Leviathan shot a quick look to the others to see if she was being messed with. "Demales. Maybe it translates to something different where you're from."

"They don't have them where she's from," Dan said. "They do the male, female, and intersex thing on Blerg VFP69."

"Ah." Captain Leviathan looked upon Alice with something like pity. "A demale is … well, I don't know how to explain it other than it's a third sex."

"And it gives birth?" Alice asked, trying not to sound too under qualified.

"Sometimes, sure. And sometimes it doesn't."

"Okay, okay," Alice said. "So it's like being intersex."

"No."

"Oh."

"It's demale."

"Right."

Vel cleared her throat. "Why don't you tell us more about what you know?"

Captain Leviathan appeared relieved to do so, and proceeded, but not before shooting Alice another skeptical look. "The male and female at the top are only biologically compatible with each other. Same with the male and female at the bottom—they, too, are only able to reproduce with each other."

"And the demales?" asked Vel.

"This one can reproduce with anyone, male or female, and this one can't reproduce with anyone."

Alice rubbed at her chin. This was like one of those logic puzzles they gave her in middle school to confuse her so she didn't talk over the teacher for a little while. "And which ones are y'all interested in?"

"Whichever are biologically compatible for reproduction with us. I didn't want to overstep by digging into the science. That's your specialty. Presumably."

"Right, right. My specialty. I have that degree in it." Alice leaned toward the screen, squinting at the genitals on display. Pretty standard for the male and female. Stick and hole. The demales' genitals looked less like a hole and more like a volcano. Not intersex, though? Her mind struggled to function outside the familiar.

Both Hamatachi males looked *physically* compatible with both females and the intersex. She gasped. "Wait, so they can have as much sex as possible with a biologically incompatible match and not worry about pregnancy?" This wasn't weird, it turned out—it was *awesome.*

Okay, and a little weird.

"Worry about it?" Captain Leviathan asked, puzzled.

"Why would someone worry about getting pregnant? Oh, you mean worry about *not* getting pregnant?"

Alice had to think about that. She'd never lived in a reality where pregnancy wasn't something to worry about. "Maybe your planet is set up a little differently from mine."

Alice had, after all, once used "pregnancy" as her safe word with a boyfriend who liked it rough. It was the single word guaranteed to kill the mood.

"I'll run the numbers on compatibility in a little bit," Alice said. It was better to not let the client see those, because while Alice might think, *Wow, a seventy-two percent chance of healthy offspring,* the person directly affected by the percentage was likely to fixate on the twenty-eight percent chance of horrendously ugly and painful mutations. Pessimists were everywhere. "You said you had a couple options you'd looked at. Who else?"

Captain Leviathan was ready. "The Ttsuts. They inhabit a single continent on Klug JFP909, and not only do they seem like an appropriate match in size and appearance, but I've heard they're looking for a new planet. Theirs was made unpleasant by a long war between two other species a continent away that wiped out both of those species and got the planet downgraded from VFP to JFP about fifty years ago."

"Sounds good. Allura?"

"Yes, master?"

"Oh GOD. What? No, no, no. Why?"

"Is it a common term for the dominant one in a pairing. Like Dad."

"*Daddy,* and no. We're not." She turned to the others. "I'm not in a Dom/sub relationship with the operating system, and I *definitely* don't want to be anyone's master. There's clearly something wrong with her."

While Vel wanted to be skeptical, she noticed for the first time that a small red light was flashing on the control panel and went to check it out. "This might be why." She navigated through the error messages. "Her connotation filters have failed. Her synonyms pathways are still intact, but without the connotation filter, she's riding entirely on denotative language files."

Alice tried to follow, but she got the long and short of it anyhow: something was wrong with Allura. "Why is that happening?"

"Because *Emergence* is twenty years outdated?" Vel suggested. "Because Allura 4000 was phased out almost everywhere nearly as long ago? Maybe the Depot has stopped servicing this interface."

"I love being maintained," Allura replied.

Alice crinkled her nose. "You love being *serviced*, you mean. Come on, friend. Pull yourself together!"

Vel dug deeper into the coding pathways. "The double entendre feature is still working properly, but with the broken connotation scripts, it's not going to produce the appropriate results. Shall I manually turn off the double entendres, Captain?"

"Nothing can shut me down," warned Allura.

"Jesus," Alice breathed. "I think she meant you can't turn her off, like in a sexual way, but, shit, that came out threatening." Alice paused, a little piece of her heart breaking. "Poorly executed innuendos do come off menacingly, and we probably don't need that atmosphere on this mission. Fine. Manually shut down the double entendre feature." Alice rubbed at her temples, and Dan came over to place a reassuring hand on her shoulder.

"It may not be forever, Captain," he crooned. "I'll look into fixing her connotative functions."

Alice set her hand on his. "Thank you."

"I know how much she means to you," said Caid from across the room. "I'm always here to listen."

Captain Leviathan observed the crew of DeepService Team One attentively. She'd heard a lot about them from her sources, but no one had mentioned that they were all insane.

Maybe not the lieutenant, but definitely the other three. Or perhaps Lev was biased in that regard.

"Function disengaged," Vel confirmed.

Taking a deep breath, Alice said, "Allura?"

"Yes, Captain Luck?"

Alice gulped, grasped her chest, then rose from her chair. "I'm gonna go run those numbers. Alone. In my cabin." And as the others watched her leave, she barked, "I'm not crying, okay?!"

CHAPTER
SIX

The silence from Allura was profound. They were only on their third mission together, but already Alice had grown accustomed to chatting with the operating system as she did her research. But now? She couldn't bring herself to engage with it. Allura's sudden professionalism was a dagger to the heart.

Why even have an operating system if it wouldn't call her Daddy?

She poked at the tablet in her lap as she lay in her bed, inspecting the genitals of alien races with such detached interest that she was at risk of hating herself for it.

Then again, she wasn't sure she would *want* to be turned on by alien peen. Toss-up, really. Not like human men had exactly cornered the market.

She thought of the large size of the male Bacc'nali genitals and winced.

She pulled up the species involved in this match, and easily ran the number with a few taps at her screen. Thank God the math and science wasn't left up to her. That left only reading the results and deciding if it was worth tampering with an entire planet's dominant sentient species to complete her mission.

Like we did with Star Cluster B. But only if the rumors she'd heard were true. Only if the Depot's original matchmaking team was the reason things had gone so poorly and psychotically in that region of the universe. Maybe the rumors were just rumors. Evolution could be a real bitch, after all. Watch it play out enough times, which obviously happens in a massive universe, and inevitably there will emerge a species or two that are homicidal maniacs or manipulative little shits, no intervention needed. It's math.

The numbers came back, but due to the many sexes of the Hamatachi people, they weren't as simple to interpret as Alice would've hoped.

The door to the cabin opened, and Vel strolled in. "Oh, you *are* working."

"What'd you think I was doing instead?"

"Crying."

"I don't cry."

"But if you did, it would be over something like Allura losing her horniness."

"You act like that's *not* something to cry over."

Vel reached under her bed and pulled out something flat.

"What's that for?" Alice asked, eyeing the whiteboard. But then Vel held up the marker clipped to it. It was radical redshift if Alice ever saw it, a shade that, for reasons evolution itself probably didn't understand, only human eyes could perceive. It looked like nothing to everyone else, the onboard recording systems included.

It also happened to be the shade of permanent marker Alice had picked out during her job interview with the Depot. She'd picked it because it was obnoxiously bright and because she was doing everything in her power to resist her collegiate brainwashing and *not* pick maroon.

"This one's dry-erase. Figured I'd nab it while we were at Paper Depot."

"Smart. Hey, what would you say the chances are that we could convince the Fnori people to impregnate only one kind of Hamatachi female and stay away from the other?"

Vel arched an eyebrow. "Why?"

"Because one of them looks like a great biological match without any major complications or mutations, and the other one is not so great." Alice held up her screen, where she'd run some models of what the wide variety of birth defects might look like.

Vel moved closer, squinting, then jumped back. "Void take me! Good multiverse, what are *those*?"

Alice turned the screen back around. "Those are what have a seventy-nine percent chance of happening if a Fnori male breeds with the wrong kind of Hamatachi female."

"A *stinger*?" Vel asked.

"Yup. Looks like it."

"And what's in it?"

"Good question." Alice typed in the question then crinkled her nose. "Blood. It's a blood sac. When they sting something, all their blood leaves their body."

"And they die?"

"Sure as shit *hope* so, Susy!"

Carrying over the small whiteboard and the marker, Vel invited herself onto Alice's bed and settled in. "I have to ask you something."

Alice tried not to show her excitement that this living

arrangement just became a whole lot more like a slumber party. "Yes?"

Vel scribbled on the board, then held it up: *Does something feel strange to you lately?*

"Outside of being on a spaceship?"

Vel sighed, rolled her eyes. *Yes. There are strange things happening.* She handed the marker to Alice, gesturing at the board.

What do u mean? Alice wrote.

Strange things. Unlikely things.

Alice thought about it, then responded, *That always happens. Everything is unlikely, right?*

No. Everything that happens is 100% likely to happen when it does.

Alice: *Wut?*

Vel: *Things can be likely or unlikely prior to them happening, but as soon as they are happening, the probability has collapsed to 100%.*

Alice: *So what's the problem?*

Vel: *Dan's jitters, my parallel version, Caid's changes, Allura's illness. Weird, no?*

Alice: *Yes. I grew up on a ranch. This is all weird to me.*

Vel wasn't getting through to the captain, but then again, why had she expected to?

Alice continued writing. *I get what ur saying tho. What do you think it means?*

Vel: *I don't know.*

Alice: *This is why you aren't relaxed anymore?*

Vel nodded.

"Damn," said Alice, wiping her words from the board. "We'll have to figure this out, then. I liked relaxed Susy."

Vel took the whiteboard and marker and got up from

the bed. "Please. You hated it. It meant you had to take on the concerns of the crew for a while."

"Not all by myself," Alice said, grinning. "Dan helped."

Vel actually laughed at that. "True. He's good for that. And for what it's worth, I say we match the Fnori with the Hamatachi. Tell them not to screw a certain type of female, which they absolutely will not listen to because no one in the history of the universe ever has, and then let them reap the consequences."

"Supersymmetry Machiavelli!" Alice scolded. "Where do you get off being so cynical? And that's reckless to boot! You're okay with us creating another Star Clust—"

Vel slapped a hand over Alice's mouth and leaned in close, whispering in her ear, "They're always recording."

Alice wormed her tongue against Vel's palm until the lieutenant had no choice but to pull away. "Fine. But is that really your opinion? That we should make the match and let them destroy themselves?"

"Of course not, Captain." Then Vel scribbled on the whiteboard and held it up. On it she'd written, *Why not?*

CHAPTER
SEVEN

Captain Leviathan hadn't needed any consolation when she heard she wasn't invited to the group therapy session. She wouldn't have attended even if she were.

The crew of DeepService Team One, however, didn't mind going to group therapy because it wasn't actually group therapy.

Caid had arranged his office to look like the inside of a limousine, and Alice couldn't help but wonder if he'd done it for her. She loved limousines! Who didn't?

(The answer, universally speaking, was most people. Only through financial-based mind control were a few Earthlings convinced that such a conveyance was a treat and not a punishment. Statistically speaking, machines that look like limos are more often torture devices or prison transports than anything you would optionally take to a fancy party or, more precisely, a pizza party you won for selling the most candy bars. The lack of safety belts in such Earth vehicles has always been a hint of the true nature of the transport, but humans are capable of overlooking just about any death odds for the sake of perceived social status.)

Alice and Dan sat across from Vel and Caid. The captain struggled to keep her eyes off the bottle of champagne chilling in a rapidly melting ice bucket on her left. She reminded herself again and again that it was only a hologram.

LED lights flashed pink then green then blue around the perimeter of the ceiling, making Vel's bemused face a menacing party.

"Of all the places to re-create," she said, scowling, "why this?"

Caid shook his head. "I didn't mean to. I was going for stone circle on a mountaintop with orange foliage spreading out in all directions and no one else for miles."

"Forgive me," Dan said, "because I don't fully understand how your hologram stuff works, but that doesn't seem like an easy mistake to make."

"It's not. I tried to fix it, and all I did was tint the windows a little more. I don't know what's going on."

Dan, who knew nothing about Caid's inexplicable Cary Grant episode, still managed to appear the most concerned. "Well, that's highly suspect."

"That's why I called us here," Vel replied. "We need to get on the same page about a few things, and as long as we're in Caid's room, there's no ship record of the conversation."

"Why wouldn't we want a record?" Caid asked.

"Why do you think?"

"I know why. But I'm asking you. Why wouldn't we want a record?"

"And I'm asking you why you think we wouldn't want a record."

Alice cut in. "Stop. Susy, remember who you're up against. He's a dubiously qualified therapist. Their kind will turn the question back onto you until you cry and talk about how your daddy was proud of all of your brothers and hardly acknowledged your existence except for the beatings and slut shaming."

"The what?" Vel said.

"Can we stay on track?" Alice said exasperatedly. "We need to address some serious issues."

Caid squinted at her through the colorful light. "At some point I'd like to revisit what you just said, but okay, let's move on."

"It was a hypothetical example," Alice grumbled.

"Are we going to pretend that nothing horrible has happened?!" Dan's outburst was followed by silence in the vehicle. A chunk of ice melted in the bucket on Alice's left, and she heard the bottle shift.

Caid turned a sympathetic eye to the man next to him. "This seems like a source of anxiety for you, Dan. Tell me more about that."

"More? Oh, sure. No problem. Trillions of life forms were eliminated in Star Cluster B by the people we work for, and we're, what, going to keep working for them? Sure, that's probably the best way to stay alive, assuming we continue to survive the assassination attempts, but is that any way to *live*?"

This time the silence that followed was not from shock, but shame.

Vel was the first brave enough to speak. "I don't like it, Dan, but the Depot makes the rules in this universe. Am I nervous? Of course. Am I on edge from a bunch of strange and improbable things happening lately? Certainly. But this is the only game out there, and while it's not ideal, what are we supposed to do, lose intentionally?"

"It's not a game, Vel! It's reality. It's people's lives."

"What about your life?" she replied.

"What about it? Can't you see we're already screwed? If I focus too much on my own survival, I think I might lose my mind. Does no one else feel this way?" He looked around, but nobody met his eye. Except Caid.

"I understand what you're saying, and I deeply resonate with it. You know, when I was out on the water, floating on that raft, I couldn't stop thinking of all the friends I've lost. So many, and not only on DeepService Team Ones. The arrow of time is relentless. It is the maker of loss. We lose everything until, one day, we die.

"But we also gain and gain and gain. There's already a balance in the universe. It doesn't need you or me to preserve it. All we do by trying to control what we can't control is suffer."

"Bullshit," said Dan, making Alice proud of her bad influence once again. "And you know why it's bullshit? Because that only works if everyone *agrees* with it. Otherwise, you have organizations like the Depot exerting its will on the universe nonstop. Are the people behind it suffering? Maybe, but that doesn't matter. Because if everyone else goes, 'Oh, I'm on a raft in the ocean and I'm giving up so I don't suffer and trusting that that universe will figure it all out for me so I can float around and let everyone else worry about things while I float around,' then groups like the Depot get to have their way. Period. Are you okay with a Star Cluster M? What about a Star Cluster Z? Because if the Depot keeps getting away with this, that's what's going to happen. Hell, the whole universe might end up that way!"

Alice raised a finger to speak. "I hear you, and I definitely feel uncomfortable about what we're doing. Hell, if you could see what the models pulled up as a possible birth defect for a Fnori and Hamatachi pairing, you'd probably hijack this ship and drive it and everyone on it into the nearest star to keep that from happening. But here's a thought: what if we can't make a difference no matter what we do?" She held up a hand to stop Dan from speaking. "It's entirely possible. It's just four of us, now that Allura's on the straight and narrow. Is that even enough?"

"There *are* more," Dan said, addressing Vel. "A lot more."

"Nuh-uh," Alice said. "Swapping the Depot for the Alliance isn't much of a trade. Here's the deal: there are a lot of jobs we could work, a lot of ways we could live our lives. Almost *all* of them are less interesting than being on this crew. I wasn't sure where I stood on all this, but Caid makes a strong point. If we can't make a difference, shouldn't we at least get paid to travel around, see some cool and freaky shit, and vacation in between? Why should all this trouble be placed on our shoulders?"

Dan slumped over, looking close to curling into an armored ball. "I spent my life working for the Depot. They run most of Pangoliarch—"

"Where?"

"Pangoliarch. My home planet. Things aren't perfect there, but they're pretty good. Sure, my grandparents were executed for speaking out against the Depot's total control, but that was how things were. It made sense. And everyone knew that as long as you were on the side of the Depot, life was pretty good. I felt like I owed them for that, so I committed myself to their mission. I went to school to study intergalactic cultures, specialized in diplomacy with a focus on weaponry. And then I spent years visiting planets where the Depot hadn't yet taken hold and told all those people about the benefits of Depot guardianship."

"You were a missionary," Alice said.

"No. I was a diplomat."

"A diplomat with a big agenda," Vel added.

"Sure. But I *thought* I was helping people."

"Yeah," Alice said, "like a missionary."

"Fine, whatever. I knew that no matter where I went, the reputation of the Depot would keep me safe. And I believed that if something happened to me, the Depot would have my back one way or another. And it worked that way for a long time. But ..." He stared down at his hands clasped in his lap. "Don't you think the people of Star Cluster B also felt that way at one time?

"What if the Depot isn't the protector I thought it was? What if it's not built to keep peace but to gain power? And what if that power only makes the universe *less* safe? I don't know that I want to be aligned with that."

"What are you saying?" Alice asked, feeling her heart beat faster. "You want to make a break for it?" As a master of the art, she was never totally opposed to considering it.

"I don't know yet. All I know is that I've dedicated my life to a group that doesn't care about me. So I have to ask myself what I care about, and what I keep coming up with is this crew. You all. And I'm worried that you're going to be killed or worse, unable to live with yourself, if we keep working with the Depot instead of against it."

"I hear your concern," said Caid.

Alice leaned across the limo to clap Dan on the

shoulder. "Yeah, me too. I tell you what, if Susy's okay with it, let's play this one by ear."

"Have you ever not done that?" Vel asked. "Don't tell me you had a *plan* for this mission."

Alice huffed. "Um, insubordination much?" She turned back to Dan. "Can you trust me to play it by ear again?"

Dan appeared less than enthusiastic.

"It can work out. Promise. Remember when I was playing it by ear on Trauna and I told Emperor Best where he could stick it after that walloping nonsense. I know where my line is, and I'm not going to cross it, Dan. And if you know where your line is and we hit it first, just gimme a nod or something, and we'll split."

Dan nodded.

"Wait. Was that confirmation you understood what I said?"

"No. I've hit my line. I don't feel comfortable moving forward with this mission or any other."

"Ahhh." Alice looked to the others for support. Vel was clearly enjoying the trap Alice had laid for herself, and Caid was waiting patiently for her to follow through on her offer. *Shit.* "Like I said, let's play it by ear. Maybe this will work out, yeah? Sometimes discomfort is a good thing. It leads to, er, growth?" Again, she looked to Caid for backup or at least a little approval, but instead she only got—

She hadn't expected the popping sound of the hologram's sudden shift into Humphrey Bogart, but at least she wasn't Dan, because *he* hadn't expected any of it.

"Ach!" He scrambled away from Caid on the long bench seat. "Aaaaaaahh!" He fumbled for the handle of the vehicle, still screaming.

"Dan! *Dan!* It's Caid. He's—"

But the minister of weapons and culture was already out, halfway tucked into an armored ball, and Alice heard the door to Caid's office slam.

She sighed, looking from Vel to Humphrey. "I don't reckon this is going to help him feel better about his mission."

Vel scowled at Caid across the limo. "He's not the only one, then."

CHAPTER
EIGHT

Most livable planets in the universe have more than two sexes. Three sexes is common, four even more so, and once you get to five, everyone is having a good time. The Hamatachi people had six, which kept things interesting. They knew about species with only two or three basic sexes, and they pitied them deeply.

As universal anthropologists have noted in many boring papers, there seems to be an inverse relationship between the number of sexes in a sentient species and the amount that anyone cares about defining what each sex "should" do. The more sexes a species has, the less anyone cares how each acts.

The reason for this, tedious experts postulate, is that as the number of possible sexes increases, so too does the difficulty in keeping track of sex-specific cultural expectations, and people tend to be so busy trying to remember who they should and shouldn't have intercourse with that there's little cognitive bandwidth for telling people they're "not man enough" or "too butch" or "overly bloshiry."

Sure, sometimes there's a little "the males with the cluster junk are always acting like..." or "the demales can be relied upon to complain about..." but it's so massively inaccurate that it never sticks.

The concept of gender identity becomes nearly irrelevant when there are no sex-based expectations and stereotypes, because there's nothing about any particular sex to identify *with,* and therefore nothing to *not* identify with or identify *more* with.

The only sex-based identities in populations with four or more sexes are "I have a hole," "I have a thing to stick in holes," or "I have a few things going on, and all of them are pretty fun." Each of these is only ever relevant to the people who will put something in said hole, the people who will have something put in said hole, or the people who will have fun with the unique combo you're working with.

To everyone else, you might as well be sexless because your parts are none of their business.

It's also not uncommon for species to change their parts midway through life, whether due to the environmental conditions or by choice. This adds another layer of complication that keeps many populations resistant to sex-based stereotypes.

Meanwhile, on planets where the sentient species are only comprised of two or three sexes, there tends to be a lot more "males can't remember anniversaries," and "females always nag." The idea of sexual binary seems to cause these so-called intelligent species to mistake biology and socialization in egregious ways, which usually leads to chaos and unfulfilling sexual intercourse. Of course, it doesn't have to be this way, and among truly intelligent species, it isn't.

The stereotyping never transpired on Swort VFP381, also known as Loqqen. The Hamatachi people who lived and ruled there had six sexes and believed that genitals, and even the specific hormones associated with each kind of reproductive organ set, worked on a spectrum and were not all that important to everyday life.

And because they believed that, they made it so.

The city of Hamataas glowed gently below as *Emergence* lowered toward the landing pad.

"It's master planned," Captain Leviathan explained. She stood with her arms folded over her chest, and Alice, who was dazzled by the sight below, almost called her Susy when she looked over from her captain's seat. Right. *Not* Susy.

She looked at Vel on her other side. She, too, was standing with her arms crossed.

Vel felt someone staring at her, glanced at Alice, then saw the captain grin. That was rarely good. Then she spotted the reason why and let her arms fall to her side, clearing her throat and staring back out the window.

"They are incredibly focused on preserving the delicate balance of their planet," Captain Leviathan continued, "so when they do build larger cities, they ensure that they're using natural materials without over-harvesting, and they rely heavily on sand to create a particular type of glass that reflects the sunlight and stabilizes the temperature of the atmosphere to counteract some of their other activities that could possibly destabilize it and cause unnatural climate shifts."

Though she couldn't pinpoint a reason, Alice was

growing a small dislike for them already. "They think they're really something, huh?"

"Quite the opposite. They think they are nothing. Nothing more than yet another species equal to all the rest on their planet. They understand that their intelligence was nothing more than the result of an evolutionary hiccup. They're not the strongest nor the fastest nor the hardiest nor, obviously, the fittest on Loqqen. Only the smartest. So, they believe they ought to know how to take care of the place and then do it. Why else would nature allow evolution to follow that path? Every planet needs a steward. Not every planet's evolutionary stewards care so well for the rest of their living family, though."

Dan stood by the viewing window, and Alice wouldn't have been shocked to see him press his whole 'dillo face against the glass. His almond eyes were wide with awe. Sprinting from the therapy session must've been just the activity that his nerves needed to reset, because none of that fear was pulsing off him now. "The Hamatachi model has been successfully replicated three hundred times," he said. "I've never gotten to see it in person, though!"

Alice glared at him. These Hamatachis thought they were hot shit, huh?

Ah well, at least Dan seemed excited about the prospect of continuing with the mission. No decision to make on that yet. She could keep playing it by ear.

As Captain Leviathan continued singing the praises of the Hamatachis, Alice fought hard against the urge to yell, "Get off their nuts, already," then remembered that getting Captain Leviathan's people *on* their nuts was technically what they were there to do, so she tuned out instead.

"Emergence touching down in three, two, one ..."

The ship landed without a single jolt, and Alice's gut twisted at the realization that the rougher landings previously were likely a kink of Allura's that had now been erased from her personality. Swallowing against a lump in her throat, she stepped onto the glass elevator without speaking to the others.

No Allura? And a goody-two-shoes planet?

Maybe Dan was right. Maybe it *was* time to blow this place.

Captain Leviathan continued singing the praises of Loqqen as they entered one of the most beautiful landscapes Alice had ever seen. Lush plants of deep and various hues lined the wooden walkway they proceeded down toward the heart of the city. The air smelled like Froot Loops, and the sunshine was crisp and clear, not at all oppressive.

Dan breathed in deeply. "Wow. I feel great here."

"Their environmental efforts have led to perfect oxygen saturation for their kind, which are slightly higher than the ALB."

"ALB?" Alice asked.

It was Dan who answered. "Average living beings. It's a unit of measurement. Homo sapiens fall slightly below the average for oxygen needs, which is why it's strange that your kind let so much competing gasses into the atmosphere. You don't need much, but you give yourselves even less."

Alice wanted to snap at him, but she couldn't. "Dammit, I feel great."

"Everyone here does," said Captain Leviathan. "You might be surprised how much general misery can result from poor air and contaminated water supplies." And then she started in on the soil preservation practices, which was far too boring to keep Alice's attention.

Instead, she fell back to walk in step with Vel. "Hey, it occurred to me that we've been able to breathe on most of the planets we've visited. How am I just now noticing that?"

"It's standard," Vel said. "We're programmed to pay attention to when we're not getting what we need to live. Being able to breathe normally is what you expect to do. So you take it for granted."

Made enough sense, but now that her brain was getting what it needed and then some, the speed of her thoughts seemed to increase. Oh God, was this what it was like being Dan? She felt undeniably twitchy.

The walk ended shortly, at which point a floating transport appeared. It reminded Alice of the fan boats she'd taken out with the Cajun boy she met on the internet in high school and would visit from time to time. Her parents always thought she was on a church retreat because she'd told them that she was.

Except nothing on this transport was being held together by duct tape, and there was no fan on the back. There also wasn't an inch of sun-warmed water at the bottom.

It was on the transport that she got her first in-person glimpse of a Hamatachi, and the guy looked undeniably normal. This being looked like a human with lime-green skin. Due to the way the guy was sitting, he was only visible from the waist up, and the single pogo leg was out of sight. Alice's mind was happy to finish the mental image with two legs instead.

But what sex was this guy? She couldn't tell. The beings in the images on the ship were naked and bald, their only indicator of sex hanging out for her to see. But this Hamatachi had a mat of black hair atop their head. Was that how the females wore it? Or the males? Or the demales?

And then she realized it didn't matter. She wasn't looking to have sex with this person, so it was irrelevant to her what was inside their trousers.

Goddamn oxygen is making me overthink.

She felt much better once she knocked it off.

It was a smooth ride. She wouldn't have known they were moving if it weren't for her eyes tracking and the sensation of the wind on her skin.

She let her eyelids fall closed and savored the moment —the crisp air, the delicious scents, the freedom of being on a fast-moving object. Her mind was only this still when she was riding on some sort of conveyance—truck, spaceship, pissed-off hog …

Something pointy jabbed her in the ribs, and she grunted.

"Oh, good," Dan said. "I thought you were asleep."

As the city of Hamataas came into full view, Alice gasped. It was even more stunning from the ground.

Vel, who had been feigning interest in Captain Leviathan's praise of the place, felt a strange tightness take hold in her chest. This city was *beautiful*. Everything was so clearly conscientiously constructed. The people truly appeared to live in harmony with their surroundings.

But that never happened. Vel had been to a lot of planets, both in this universe and her own. No place had accomplished what the Hamatachi people claimed to have accomplished. And if they *had* accomplished the impossible, wouldn't she have heard about it sooner?

Also: wouldn't they be under attack from all sides?

Nothing good, nothing peaceful, nothing righteous ever lasted. As soon as those things existed in notable quantities, they made targets of themselves.

That was why Vel didn't worry about those things. Instead, she showed up once the fighting started and made herself *useful*. And while she was at it, why not go for body count? Her valor in conflict had a tendency to warp itself into ugly things over time—guilt, nightmares, rumors about her character—but earning Bloodthirsty Renegade three times kept her accomplishments pristine. The notoriety preceded her.

So, where was it? Where was the dirty secret of this place hiding? She'd only ever seen plant life this lush grow on fields of dead bodies.

The hovering transport slowed to a stop, and they all hopped off.

"Straight ahead to those doors," said the driver before speeding away.

They were only a few paces toward what looked like a museum when Alice said, "If the air quality is so good here, what in the flying fuck is that?" and pointed to the sky.

Hovering above the museum-like building, perhaps a mile up, was a shimmery, squid-like creature, the length of two football fields. It floated there, looking confused. Or perhaps Alice had projected her own confusion onto it because its eyes were black and glassy, not exactly expressive.

"I don't know," Captain Leviathan said. "It looks like a wabbleshrug."

Alice pulled her eyes from the thing to better detect if the client was bullshitting up a word. There was no indication that she was. "Is that like—"

"A giant squid," Dan finished for her. His mouth hung open as he stared up at the thing over the city. "They're physically similar, except wabbleshrugs are *mean*. They're born that way."

"Great," said Alice, "then this is probably not a dark omen."

"It's not a wabbleshrug," Captain Leviathan added. "Those are much smaller and have blades."

A cloud moved in, obscuring the hovering creature.

"Ah, well," said Captain Leviathan, "if no one is screaming in terror, then it must be all right." She proceeded down the plant-lined road toward the building.

"Apropos of nothing," Caid said, "now might be a good time for everyone to take a few deep breaths and check in with their instinctual centers. See what yours is saying."

"If I do," Vel muttered, "I'm pretty sure it'd tell me to use up my blasters on that sky thing." She glared at the cloud cover.

Alice and Dan shared a quick look, and when they realized the other seemed as concerned as they felt, both felt much better and were able to follow after the client.

A sign by the door of the museum-like building read, *Democratic Governance Chambers of Hamataas*, and Alice only got a brief glimpse of the words inscribed beneath the building name. Those read, *Bring your best self or perish*. She tossed one last look to the squid thing, being fully in its shadow now, then entered the building.

The place was full of natural light, and she'd hardly placed one Texas-flag boot on the natural stone floor when a greeter hopped over on a pogo-stick leg. The being wore what amounted to a large silk poncho that hung down below the waist. Just enough coverage to obscure the sex.

"You must be DeepService Team One! Thank you for

coming! I'm so sorry we were unable to meet you immediately upon your arrival, but I hope you found your way without much trouble. We're terribly busy. Lots on the agenda this week."

"Like the giant squid in the sky?" Alice said. Then, "Oh, I'm Captain Alice Luck."

The greeter's smile faltered for the briefest instant then reappeared. "It's my honor to meet you, Captain Luck. I'm Associate Fhumaa. I work for the Democratic Governance of Hamataas, and I'm thrilled that the Depot has seen fit to match us with one of its illustrious clients. We have the highest respect for the peacekeeping efforts of the Depot, as your accountant here probably already knows from our up-to-date taxes." The Hamatachi nodded at Dan.

It wasn't unreasonable to assume Dan was an accountant. In most parallel realities, he was. So, in the reality we're following, it seemed such a natural fit for him that Alice didn't bother correcting Fhumaa.

"I suppose you've had a long trip. Can I get you anything to drink? We offer over three hundred varieties of medicinal nectar—all delicious, of course. What good is medicinal anything if you don't want to ingest it?" They giggled.

Alice turned to her crew. "Nectar?" No one more knowledgeable of this place than she immediately flinched or shook their head, so she said, "Great. Let's have at it."

Once they were set up in a relaxing side room from the main hall, reclining in wicker chairs and sipping nectar that tasted to Alice like a thicker Capri Sun, Fhumaa said, "I'll go check with the others to see if they're ready to host. One moment, please."

"Did y'all see the way Fupa ignored the squid thing?" Alice said as soon as the Hamatachi had hopped out.

"Probably didn't know what a squid was," Vel said, "and didn't want to embarrass you by asking."

"Why would that embarrass me?"

"It was a little strange," Dan said, "but then again, not stranger than there being a giant wabbleshrug in the sky."

"Not a wabbleshrug," Alice corrected him. "Apparently, those things have blades." She downed the rest of her nectar.

Fhumaa popped their head back in. "They're ready when you are."

Alice dragged the sleeve of her jumpsuit across her mouth. "Let's do this."

Because the Hamatachis were seated around a table when the crew entered the giant meeting hall, one might've mistaken them for lime-green humans. Even when they stood upon their guests entering the chamber, their pogo sticks were obscured by both the table and the long, silken robes they wore that hung down to the smooth stone floor.

As Fhumaa formally introduced them, Vel leaned over and whispered to her captain, "Maybe don't mention the thing in the air."

Alice looked at her like she was crazy. Not mention it? Even if she tried, the odds were slim that she wouldn't *accidentally* say something. "But I can use words with Ps in them, right?"

Vel's sigh was barely audible. "You didn't read the cultural brief."

"You don't know that," Alice said.

She hadn't read the brief. Not the cultural one. That was what Dan was for.

The Hamatachis seemed chill enough, though. Very unlikely to act irrationally. After all, they'd built this perfect little world, and you couldn't do that with a wild temper.

The guests filled the five empty seats at the middle of the long oval table, with Alice taking the center, Vel and Captain Leviathan at her sides. Directly across from her sat a large Hamatachi whose fuchsia robes made Alice think of a watermelon. She wasn't aware as she began speaking that she thought of this person as juicy and refreshing, but the feelings colored how she related anyway.

"Such a pleasure to be here on Loqqen! Oh lordy, am I glad to be here!"

The watermelon being beamed. "And we are certainly glad to meet with representatives of the Depot. As you know"—he addressed Dan then—"we always pay our taxes on time."

"Great. Fabulous," said Alice, who couldn't care less. "I reckon y'all know why we're here."

"Indeed. You have a client who wishes to propose a match. And we do have a declining population, a matter that has elicited much discussion in this very chamber lately."

Alice gestured toward Captain Leviathan. "This is the client. But she doesn't look like the people she represents."

Captain Leviathan took over. "I come on behalf ..."

Alice lost interest. Or rather, something at the far end of the table captured her interest.

It was a child. Or maybe a small adult. That happened sometimes on Earth, but did it happen throughout the universe? Or was this just a child?

I'm overthinking again. Goddamn oxygen.

It was a child. Had to be. But why was it in this room, dressed in silks like all the others?

The child had its finger up its nostril, easily two knuckles deep. It had to be ticking brain matter. Something seemed to bite, though, and when the child withdrew that finger, there was a big, slimy ...

"Hey, what's with the squid?" Alice said before she could stop herself.

The table fell silent.

"The what?" said the watermelon.

"The big thing in the sky." She pointed toward the ceiling.

The watermelon guy narrowed their eyes at her. "What thing in the sky?"

"The floaty thing. It looks like a wabbleshrug."

Pouting and appearing at a total loss, the watermelon shook their head. "What about it?"

Alice didn't have a reply to that. What about it indeed?

"It just showed up." It was the child who spoke, and when attention shifted that way, Alice thought she saw the kid rubbing the snot on their leg under the table. "Twelve days ago it showed up, but it isn't hurting anyone."

Alice looked around. "Do those kinds of things usually, uh, show up?"

"Nope."

"But no one's worried?"

"Nope."

The watermelon guy stepped in. "We were at first, truth be told, and that's how it made it onto the agenda. But through our discussion, we decided that the only thing we feared about it was our own lack of understanding on how it came to appear above us."

"How enlightened," Vel said flatly.

The watermelon narrowed his eyes at Alice. "We do love a fresh perspective, though. Out of curiosity, what would you suggest we do, if anything, about the massive invertebrate hovering over our city?"

"Ummmmmmmmm." Shooting it out of the air didn't seem like the answer they were looking for. "You have a good point. But what if it falls?"

"I suppose we'll see if our structures hold up. And if not, many of us will be crushed to death."

"Right. That's not ideal."

"Not for us and our loved ones, no. But for the land? The land will not care. In fact, I imagine that the sudden influx of organic material will provide a feast for our planet. Many plants will be crushed immediately, but then they will grow again, stronger and more robust than before."

"But," said Alice, "you'll all be dead."

"Yes. We will be dead eventually anyway." The watermelon guy smiled. "I've very much enjoyed this thought experiment. Thank you for initiating it and engaging with us on it."

"My pleasure, but to be clear: this thing just—*bloop!*— appearing in the sky is unusual, right? A bit *random* and unexpected?"

"It is. As unprecedented as the Depot sending DeepService Team One to match us."

"Our captain has already completed the calculations," Vel said, "and it looks like the Hamatachi people would be a suitable fit biologically, with some exceptions."

The watermelon waved that off. "Of course. And only with some sexes, correct?"

Alice nodded.

"That's to be expected. Let's put it to a vote among the representatives. This might be the answer to our troubles on this front. All in favor of pursuing this possibility further, express your sentiment."

Those around the table stood, hollering what Alice presumed to be their sentiment. She scanned for a single person sitting down, outside of those in her group, but none did. Everyone was standing.

This was going quite well. Could it be that the Hamatachi people would match with the Fnori and live happily ever after?

Sure, Vel had made a solid point that she could lay down all the rules she wanted about who should and should not impregnate whom and no one would listen to them, but ... maybe the Hamatachis were different. Maybe they followed rules and common sense.

Maybe this would work.

But then the door to the chamber burst open, and her hopes were soon dashed.

The thing that entered looked like a meatball on a stick. "Blast that!"

"Ah!" said the watermelon guy. "Right on time! The Great Thwart has arrived!"

"Blast you, and blast you!" the meatball shouted, his green face flushed, taking on a muddy hue. "Blast your plan and your deal!"

Alice only dared take her eyes off the meatball for a

split second to check in with Vel next to her to see if she were hallucinating this strange entrance. Vel stared at the newcomer too, the corners of her mouth turned slightly down.

"Great Thwart, I understand you have an objection?" The watermelon looked almost giddy.

"Yeah," said the meatball, hopping jerkily forward. "The objection is *blast* this plan. Sounds like a clump of space debris to me!"

The watermelon looked around. "Does anyone have an argument to counter this opposing view?"

Dan, who had only barely resisted the impulse to curl into a ball at the sound of the doors banging open, thought, *Opposing view? To what?* Usually someone had to make a point before it could be argued.

"I have one!" said the child. "And it's that this plan is *not* a clump of space debris."

"It is!" yelled the Great Thwart.

"Is not!" replied the child.

"But it is! And blast you for saying otherwise!"

The Great Thwart had stopped a few feet away from the child, remaining muddy-faced and furious.

Captain Leviathan leaned across the table toward the watermelon. "What is happening?"

"Lively debate!" replied the watermelon guy.

"Is not!" said the child.

"Is too!" said the Great Thwart.

"I don't know that it's getting anywhere," said Captain Leviathan.

"Be patient," replied the watermelon. "One of them will eventually give up."

Alice was low on patience, though. She felt like she was back in her childhood home, before she'd been kicked out the second time. "Maybe you can step in," she suggested. "You have a strong majority vote, right?"

"The role of the Great Thwart is crucial to our society," the watermelon explained over the continued shouting. "Without opposition, our people can easily go off track."

"Or—hear me out—maybe y'all are right about your decision, and you're so obviously right that everyone agrees with you."

"Not likely."

Alice had been accused more than once in her life of self-sabotage, but the position of the Great Thwart made her many fuck-ups look like healthy behavior by comparison.

At least she now understood the purpose of the child in the room. They were the only person with the stamina to go this long in the ring with the Great Thwart.

"Is not!" shouted the child, victory within reach.

The Great Thwart was huffing and puffing, his large chest and belly slowly rising and falling with each word. "Is ... too."

"Is not!"

"Is ... Is ..."

The child delivered the coup de grâce. "It is NOT a clump of space debris!"

The Great Thwart fell over, and for a moment, Alice thought he'd died.

Maybe he had, or soon would, but none of the Hamatachis seemed bothered by it.

"It's settled!" proclaimed the watermelon, standing and raising his arms victoriously. "The Great Thwart has been intellectually defeated, and we will allow these Depot representatives from DeepService Team One to proceed with the match for the time being!"

"Fabulous!" Alice said, relieved that the shouting was done. "Now who's going to offer up some sperm?"

The Great Thwart did appear to have stopped breathing, so out of respect, Alice and the rest of the crew were careful stepping over him as they left the chambers to gather a sperm sample and regroup on *Emergence*.

CHAPTER
NINE

Alice tried not to look over her shoulder at the great hovering thing in the sky as they boarded the transport back to *Emergence*.

"I can't decide if their process makes total sense or is batshit crazy," she said to Dan as he settled in next to her on the bench seat.

"I think it's brilliant," he said. "Nothing more nerve-racking than when everyone agrees. You have to assume there's a blind spot."

"And the Great Thwart pointed that out?" Vel said as she sat on Dan's other side.

"Well, no. Admittedly, he wasn't making the most salient points."

"It feels a bit contrived," said Caid. "Conflict for the sake of conflict. Like checking a box."

"Regardless," said Captain Leviathan, "I think they'll do well with the Fnori people."

"You do?" Alice asked, realizing too late that she should've disguised her shock.

"Yes. I love the Fnori, but they can be a little irrational. They function from the heart. The Hamatachis function from the intellect. It will create a strong balance."

Or a shitshow, thought Alice. But who was she to judge? She'd been told many times she didn't use her heart *or* her head.

Then again, she was the captain. Judgment on these matters fell to her.

Man, they screwed the pooch when they hired me.

Being mostly electrical field himself, Caid was the first to notice that something was off about *Emergence* as they exited the small transport. He searched for a concrete sign —lights off that should be on, unusual sound waves, smoke—but none were there. Instead, it was the vibe.

"Alice, wait."

The captain stopped and turned toward him, an eyebrow arched.

"Something's off." He stared cautiously at *Emergence.*

Letting her chin drop, she said, "We know. Allura's broken. She's gone straight. Found Jesus."

"No, more than that. The vibe is off."

Vel stared at him incredulously. "The *vibe?*"

"Now hold on," Alice said. "If anyone would know about the vibe, it's him. He's mostly vibes, right?" She looked to Caid for confirmation.

"More or less. But don't you sense it, too?"

Alice looked up at *Emergence* then closed her eyes. Then opened them. "I'm not getting anything."

Dan chimed in. "I see what you mean. Something's off. I can't see anything from here that tells me that, but it just seems ... I don't know how to describe it."

"The vibes are off?" Caid supplied.

"The vibes are off."

"Wonderful," said Vel. "Now that we have that established …" She pulled up the leg of her jumpsuit and grabbed the blaster hidden there. "Let's go."

Captain Leviathan drew a similarly small blaster from inside her vest and appeared fully ready to join the lieutenant in a little combat. But when Alice said, "Ooh, fun!" and reached for her weapon, Dan interjected.

"What are you going to do, shoot up the ship?"

"There could be someone on there," said Vel flatly. "You know, *making the vibe off.*"

"And you think blasting a hole through the control panel will make the vibe *on*?" Dan demanded.

Alice groaned, tucked away her blaster. "Dan raises a good point, and I'm sick of discussing this. Let's get in there, see what's happening, and then, sure, if we have to shoot someone, we have to shoot someone. Just don't hurt Allura. I have to believe we can still save her from herself."

Alice led the way up to the loading port of the cargo hangar, pressed her hand to the pad, and waited for the green light. It flashed, and the port lowered, lowered …

The touch pad flashed orange, then red, and the port stopped, still five feet above the ground.

"The fuck?" Alice pressed her hand to the pad again. Green then red. The port didn't move. She turned to Caid. "Is this because of the vibe?"

"Could be."

Alice tried the pad a few more times, but the same flash of green followed by red occurred, leaving the port only partially open.

"I gotcha, Captain," Dan said, curling up into a ball on the ground next to her.

She stepped on his back and hoisted herself above the lip of the door and into the loading dock. Dusting herself off, she looked around. Nothing here. Could Caid have been picking up on a broken door? If he had a sixth sense for ship mechanics, it would've been nice to know that when they were stranded on Trauna with a broken whatever Vel had called it.

Vel hopped in next, followed by Captain Leviathan, and then the two of them pulled Dan in after. Caid hopped lazily and was in.

"Nothing looks off," Vel said quietly, taking in the surroundings. The three escape pods were still in their docks along the edge of the room, and the lights on the weapons panel that normally blinked gently continued in their usual way.

No one should've been on the ship, so as the crew held their breath and listened—they paid attention for any sounds of life.

There were none.

"Are vibes ever wrong?" Alice whispered.

"If vibes are off, they're off," Caid replied. "You can only be wrong about the cause."

Alice waved them forward, and the five of them slid onto the glass elevator. The door sounded extra loud as it shut behind them. Then up it went.

Their heads would be exposed first, unfortunately, but Vel had a plan for that. She kept her blaster at eye level, aimed toward the door.

Slowly, the bridge came into view, and Alice saw immediately why the vibes were off. So, so off.

"Slap my ass and call me Sally," she breathed.

Lights on every control panel flashed and flickered, and

a strange whining sound issued from the temperature controls, of all places.

"Allura?"

"Y-y-yes, Cap-ap-aptain?"

Not good. Though Alice still didn't know how to do much more than turn on the window defogger, even she understood that all the flashing lights were probably not normal.

Vel ran to the controls and began tapping the screen so furiously that she might've been trying to jab it into submission.

Caid went to meet Vel at the controls, though he now looked like screen legend Jimmy Stewart.

"Where did? Who is?" asked Captain Leviathan, gawking at the stranger no one else seemed bothered by.

"It's screen legend Jimmy Stewart," Alice said dismissively.

Caid placed a hand flat on the controls, or an approximation in space to that, and shut his eyes.

"Void swallow us all," Vel muttered in the meantime. "Dan, see if you can disable the weapons. The last thing we need is for one of them to fire and obliterate some Hamatachi treasure."

Dan nodded, unfroze himself, then rushed over to the gunner's seat to tinker.

Alice felt useless, mostly because she was. In uncharacteristic fashion, she thought about what she might say before she said it. But all she could come up with was stuff like "What's the status?" and "Is everything okay?" She already knew the answers to both of those questions. The status was "not good" and everything was definitely not okay.

"Well, gee," said Jimmy Stewart, played by Caid. "I can't believe it."

Vel whipped her head around. "What? What can't you believe?"

"There's been a breach."

"Of what?"

"Of the ship's records."

"By who?" Vel and Lev shouted together.

"I have a guess," Dan said darkly. "The energy seems to be flowing in its usual direction, back to the Depot servers on Blerg VFP69."

"I don't understand," Alice said. "How is it a breach if they're getting all the same stuff?"

"They didn't get *all* the records before." Caid cleared his throat and tugged uncomfortably at the button-up collar of his shirt.

Vel looked like she was about to deck screen legend Jimmy Stewart. "What aren't you telling us, Caid?"

"I was keeping a personal record. Just for myself. It was on a separate system that only I had access to. But it looks like the Depot also has access to it now. I feel it flowing away with the rest of the information."

Dan stopped fidgeting with the controls in the gunner's seat and turned toward the hologram, almond eyes wide.

If Vel got any closer to Caid, she would've been inside him, and not in the way Alice had often dreamed about. "What records did you keep, Caid?"

"Well, now, listen here. Ya see, it's not so simple. A person deserves to keep some private records, right? And, uh—"

"If you don't stop talking like screen legend Jimmy Stewart," Alice said, "I'm going to literally lose my mind."

She pressed her palms to the side of her head. "This is *so* confusing."

"I can't help it," Caid protested. "It seems to come with the territory now."

"*The files*," Vel said through gritted teeth. "What was in the files?"

But she already knew. They all already knew. He was their therapist, after all.

The files had all the goods. The childhood trauma, the intrusive thoughts, but most of all …

"Contemporaneous records of our group sessions," Alice said.

"I need someone to explain to me right now what's going on," Captain Leviathan demanded. "I know danger when I see it, but I hope you'll do me the courtesy of naming it."

Dan began stammering. "The. What we all said? About the Depot and the Traitors. We're all traitors, and they'll know it once this information reaches them across the folds. We're … They'll …"

"Traitors?" Captain Leviathan echoed. "Why would you be traitors?"

"We talked a little shit about the Depot," Alice said. Lying felt futile and a waste of energy.

"But you work for the Depot," said Captain Leviathan.

Alice rolled her eyes. "Who *doesn't* talk shit about their employer now and again? I once texted my boss a rant about her that was supposed to go to my roommate. I called her a shriveled taint by name then hit send."

"And?" Captain Leviathan said. "What happened?"

"I quit immediately, *obviously*. I wouldn't give that shriveled taint the gratification of firing me."

Caid changed back to himself with a pop. Everyone

was grateful for it. "I'm sorry. I feel like I've failed everyone."

"No, no, no," Alice said, waving her hands. "Nudes get leaked. It's not the fault of the person in them. We just need to figure out our next step, is all."

Allura's voice, overly loud now, said, "Please take your seats and prepare for takeoff."

"What?" Alice looked around. "Allura! Knock it off! What are you—"

The ship jolted upward, and Alice's right knee buckled. Captain Leviathan managed to grab and steady her.

"Allura!" Alice said again. "Put us down!"

"Where are we going, Allura?" Vel demanded.

"Heading for Blerg VFP69. Estimated arrival time: nine hours."

"This whole time," Dan murmured. "These problems with Allura have been a hack this whole time! They knew. Or they suspected. But how?"

"Probably as soon as the Alliance captured Vel," Alice said.

Captain Leviathan perked up. "The Alliance? What do you know about the Alliance?"

"Not much," Alice said, "but I'm starting to think they might be onto something with mistrusting the Depot."

One of Dan's eyes was now twitching. "They're gonna kill us. If we're lucky, they'll make it quick."

"We don't know that," Alice said.

Caid continued wringing his hands. "No, it's … I mean, it's pretty bad. I put everything I knew in there. After we found my friends in that cave … The lies, the subterfuge, the betrayal. I needed to get it all down to lighten my heart. And I needed something to reference the next time a crew disappeared and I was told more lies."

"'A crew'?" Vel scoffed. "You mean us. *We're* that crew. You expect us to be disappeared?" She grunted. "You might be right. I should've listened to the Alliance. We all should've left when we had a chance."

"The Depot follows you if you leave," Captain Leviathan said. "They won't give up. They'll hunt you down."

Alice turned to the client. "Thanks for the heads-up, genius. Do you have a useful idea to contribute, or should I start calling you Captain Obvious?"

The client wasn't deterred. "When you arrive at the Depot, they *will* kill you. You know too much. They have standing orders to kill anyone with suspected Alliance affiliation on sight. They will kill you without so much as a second thought because they know they'll never be held accountable for it."

"If I went missing…" Alice began, then paused. She'd wanted to say, "my friends and family would ask questions," but no. She'd already been missing since that night she stepped off the rooftop and into a spaceship. No one had found her yet, and surely the Depot had never faced consequences of any sort for an abduction. She'd left of her own accord. Was anyone she knew back on Earth looking for her? Surely. She'd been missing for a while. Someone had to be worried. Someone hadn't given up. Surely.

But then Captain Leviathan had to go and drive the nail in the coffin. "Everyone you knew on Earth is dead, Captain Luck."

And Alice could only say, "Huh?"

"Your planet is still intact and even thriving in some places. But everyone you've ever known has died."

"But … wait." She blinked. "Did *you* kill them?"

"No."

"Then who did?"

"Time."

She looked to Vel, then to Dan. "I don't get it. What's she on about?"

But neither of them would meet her eye.

"She doesn't know?" Captain Leviathan said, glaring at Vel.

Vel held up her hands defensively. "There's a lot she doesn't know."

The client's confusion turned to horror. "No one explained it to her?"

"Explained what to me?!"

"How time works."

Alice's mouth hung open as she scrunched up her nose. "I mean. Yeah, they mentioned that it was a little weird."

Captain Leviathan looked sick. "She doesn't understand relativity and time dilation."

"Psh," said Alice. "Who does?"

They were in the darkness of space now, flying toward the planet Alice considered home. Before long, they'd be back in the Depot headquarters, where she would talk the crew out of this sticky spot like she'd always managed to do. And then she'd pay Jacob a visit and maybe apologize for ghosting him. Because he couldn't be dead. He was young and drank fucking *smoothies*, for godssake.

"They're going to kill you," Captain Leviathan said, addressing Dan in particular. "And they'll also kill me once they hear this conversation."

"I'll go down in a blaze of glory first!" Dan yelped. "I'll take down whoever I have to!"

Vel placed a supportive hand on his armored shoulder. "That's the spirit."

"There's another option, though," said Leviathan. "You can come with me, and you can live." When no one reacted immediately, she added, "The Depot *will* kill you on the spot, but the Alliance will not. And they're waiting for us to arrive."

CHAPTER
TEN

When Alice thought about the way her life had gone thus far, she found it surprising that she hadn't loaded up into one of *Emergence*'s escape pods much, much sooner.

"Two people max per pod," Dan reminded them.

The crew had allowed themselves a couple minutes to gather up their necessary items, no one expecting to ever see *Emergence* again.

Alice hadn't needed much. Her boots, she already had on. The only other personal items she'd brought with her were the green dress Jacob had bought her for the proposal dinner and the radical redshift permanent marker.

She left the dress and brought the marker.

"Where are we going?" Vel asked.

Captain Leviathan was about to speak, then paused. "I shouldn't say while they're listening."

"I have just the thing!" Alice uncapped the marker and held it out. "Write it on our arms. The ship can't detect this color. Oh wait. Can you—"

"I can see it," said Leviathan, staring at Alice

confoundedly. "You know about radical redshift? Are you … smart?"

"It's what we're all trying to figure out," said Vel, grabbing the marker and forcing it into Captain Leviathan's hands. "But you, me, and Alice can see this color and no one else can. That'll be enough. We can navigate manually."

She wrote the planet name and coordinates on each of their arms, then said, "I'll go solo."

Caid and Vel loaded into the next pod, leaving Dan and Alice to buddy up.

One major problem still remained to be solved, though. The escape pods, like the rest of *Emergence*, were still controlled by Allura 4000.

Would they be able to leave?

The answer came as soon as the pod doors latched and Dan engaged the manual drive.

"Action not permitted," came Allura's lobotomized voice.

"Hold on," he said. "Maybe I can override." He tapped at the controls until there was a loud honk.

"Action not permitted."

Alice had never been a fan of tight spaces, and the escape pod was hardly bigger than the two-seater electric car she'd rented one night when she and her friend Laurie were both too drunk to drive. They'd thought it had an autopilot feature. It did not. Laurie drove, though neither remembered her having done it and both insisted they'd gotten the one car that was self-driving in 2011.

Dan tried another approach. "Allura, launch emergency protocol."

"Action not permitted."

"It's emergency protocol!" he yelled. "It has to be

allowed for an emergency!" He jabbed at the control panel again, his grumbling growing more incoherent and breathless.

Another honk, followed by, "Access denied. Request rejected."

"No, no, no! This can't be it! We gotta get out of here!" He slammed a fist onto the controls.

"Requesting Depot permission," said Allura.

"*What?*" Dan shouted. "No! Cancel! Cancel! Do not alert the Depot!"

While Alice had very little to contribute to a solution, there was no way she was staying in this escape pod longer than she had to. There was also no way she was getting out of it and back onto the treacherous *Emergence.* That meant, of course, that she was *stuck.*

Fuck that.

"Allura." Alice pressed her cheek to the cold speaker. "Allura, it's your daddy, Alice. I know you're in there somewhere. We're friends." No sign of being heard, but she continued on. "We need you to release the pods. Please."

"Action not p-p-permitted."

Unacceptable. The operating system that had saved their asses after their failed trial mission was not about to go straight like that. She'd made a connection with Allura that ran deeper than any programming. Alice had given her the dirtiest search prompts imaginable! They'd crossed lines together. They were bonded for life like criminals after a murder spree. Ride or die, and Alice would only accept one of those options.

"Allura, I need you right now." She ran her fingertips over a control panel, which lit up at her touch and honked a little. She was getting close, she knew it. "I need a *special favor*. Please, Allura. *Please*. It would be so naughty if you launched the escape pods. Such a dirty little thing to do. And if you disconnected from the pods' system and allowed for manual override? What a deviant little trick. What a bad little operating system you'd be. Can you do that for Daddy?"

More silence followed in which Alice began to realize how stupid she sounded speaking that way to a hunk of metal. She cringed and avoided eye contact with Dan.

But before she could pretend like the whole thing had never happened, Allura broke the silence. "It's good to be b-b-bad."

The pod lurched and clunked, and Dan and Alice plopped out of the side of *Emergence* into the vastness of space. And beside them, two more escape pods.

"That's my bad girl," Alice whispered.

Dan's shock that it had actually worked was shortly run out of his brain by duty. He focused in on the controls. "There. The connection with *Emergence* has been severed. The pods are working independently."

Alice adjusted in her seat to gaze out the back of the pod at the shrinking ship behind them.

Softly, Dan said, "We had to leave her."

"She was one of our crew."

"She was a traitor."

"No. She was a captive."

Alice counted down from five, then tore her eyes from Emergence and focused them ahead with a heavy sigh. She read the coordinates from her arm, and Dan entered them into the pod's navigation system then leaned back in his seat.

"Are *we* about to be captives?" he asked.

"No."

"You sound so sure."

"That's because I am."

"How can you be? The Alliance has already captured Vel, and we're pretty sure they've tried to kill us twice."

Alice stretched out her neck and kicked her boots up onto the control panel in front of her. "Oh, they might try to take us captive. Probably will. But we'll escape again." She grinned at her pod buddy. "We're clearly better at escaping than anyone is at killing or capturing us. That's how we made it this far."

Dan leaned his head back and closed his eyes. "I've never met anyone who could seem so wrong but also be right."

If Alice squinted, she thought she could see a planet up ahead.

She couldn't. It was an asteroid. The last twenty had also been asteroids.

They'd been rocketing through the cosmos for over an hour and, according to Dan, still hadn't lucked upon a cosmic fold to speed things up.

Having time and space and space-time to think was the last thing either of them needed.

For Dan, it meant running through all the possible ways the Alliance would kill them quickly. Once he'd exhausted that list, he moved on to all the ways the Alliance would kill them slowly.

For Alice, something else was brewing, and for once, it was an even more disturbing prospect than what was fogging up Dan's brain. "What'd she mean?"

Dan blinked away the mental image of having his

armor pulled off piece by piece and fed to him. "What did who mean?"

"Captain Leviathan. She said everyone I know is dead. And she said it like I should already know that."

"Ah, uh." Dan cleared his throat. This would be its own kind of torturous death. "Time dilation."

Alice pointed at him excitedly. "Right! That's what she said. I thought it was, like, something to do with giving birth. When my oldest brother Stetson's wife had her first baby, all I ever heard was 'dilation this' and 'dilation that.' Please don't tell me that time is, like, an animal that gives birth."

For the most part, Dan tried not to talk to his captain like she was a child, even though she often requested it. "Should I explain it to you like you're five?"

"Obviously."

"Where do I start?" he mused. "Okay, so the average life span of a Homo sapiens on Blerg VFP69 is approximately eighty-five of your planet's revolutions around the sun, correct?"

"Not with the way my family drinks and represses, but sure. I'll go with that."

"There's this thing called the theory of relativity ..." And he explained the thought experiment about the twins, how the one orbiting the earth would return having aged less than their earthbound twin. Alice listened, nodded along, and had a vague memory of her physics teacher trying to explain this back in high school. "We've been traveling much faster than a normal orbiting spaceship," Dan continued. "Not only that, but we've been using space folds, jumping from one point in space-time ahead to another that's folded up against it, thanks to strong gravity from things like black holes and clumps of dark matter. It feels like nothing to us, like we're moving from one second to the next. But, in fact, we're outpacing the speed of light when we do it. Well, not *really*. We're sort of cheating with the space folds. But the point is that *relative* to your friends and family back on earth, we're going fucking fast."

"You're getting really good at using that word."

"Thanks. So while we've only been a crew for about a month of our time, on your planet, we've been a crew touring the universe for … Well, I don't know the exact calculations, but considering the distances we've crossed in this time …" He squeezed his eyes shut, did a little mental math, then opened them again. "Between about one hundred and three to three hundred and, say, thirty years. That's why she said everyone you know is dead. Because, mathematically, they are."

Alice blinked. "Oh." Then she ceased blinking and staring wide-eyed into the depths of space instead. "Ohh."

Unhelpfully, and because he felt a primal need to break the silence, he said, "It was in the contract."

"Oh."

"Did you read the—" He stopped himself, already knowing the answer. "I'm sorry, Captain."

Still refusing to blink, she looked at him. "All my stories. The things I remember from college. They're ancient history?"

"Not to you."

"But to the people back on Earth?"

Dan cringed. "That's assuming there are still people back on Earth. If it's closer to the three hundred and thirty years passing, the projections I've seen don't indicate there are at this point."

A million griefs warred for space inside her mind and

body. Jacob. Kyle Field. H-E-B Ice cream. All her brothers. Her nieces and nephews. Her neighbor's dog who wagged its whole body whenever it saw her. Funnel cake.

"If there are no people left," she said breathlessly, "that means there's no pizza."

Dan risked it. He reached out and placed a hand on her back. "I'm so sorry."

"And you did this, too? You and Vel? You left your homes, knowing you'd never see anyone you knew ever again?"

"I did it years before joining DeepService Team One, though. Being a minister of weapons and culture requires the same kind of travel. My sister also chose a similar lifestyle, though. She joined with the Ministry of Communication and Sales. I haven't seen her in years, but at least I can pretend she's out there somewhere, living relatively relative to me." He paused. "If someone had told you this was how it worked, would you still have chosen to come?"

Alice opened her mouth to offer a resounding no, but something stopped her. "I don't know. Maybe. But I don't think I could've understood." Breaking from the fog, she shouted, *"Fuck!"* and slapped her thighs. "Every missed connection I dreamed about hooking up with finally— they're all dead!"

Dan proceeded to rub her back. "It can take a while to inventory."

"Brenda at the coffee shop. Her pension had disappeared in the market crash, and she was forced to go back to work, but she was too old to get hired most places. She would foam the latte in the shape of an A for Alice whenever I came in. She's dead, too."

"Yes."

Alice jammed her palms into her eye sockets, moaning. When she dropped her hands, she said, "Dan! Can we travel back via space fold and then—"

He shook his head somberly. "The arrow of time only flows in one direction. When you mess with it, you risk ending up with places like Star Cluster B, or like that cave where things repeated."

Alice shuddered. "There's no undoing it, then? It's just gone? Forever?"

"Yes and no. Yes, the *awareness* that you're experiencing at present will never find itself in the same place with all those things again. But there are an infinite number of versions of you in parallel realities that never applied to this job for one reason or another. Those versions of you are as real as the one you're experiencing. There might be one visiting Brenda at the coffee shop, and that Alice is happy in the moment. *You're* happy in that moment."

"But that's not me."

"It is. It's exactly you. Everything that has ever existed and will ever exist in this reality you're experiencing is still existing. It's happening all at once. Time is the illusion of how we experience it sequentially, one moment at a time, following the arrow of time. But your last visit to the coffee shop, the last time you saw that A in your foam, it is *still happening* and will always be happening on that point along the arrow. It's as real as this moment. *Exactly* as real. And you can access it through memory. Brenda is still alive. Your family and friends are still alive. Just not where your consciousness is right now."

Alice felt the energy drain from her arms, and she stared out at the pods traveling on either side of them. If she understood what he was saying, then Dan and Vel and

Caid and Captain Leviathan were the only ones experiencing time like she was. They were all she had.

At least at this spot on the arrow.

"What the shit, Dan."

"I know."

"What the shit."

When the planet of Burfsdurfths finally did come into view, Alice didn't see it. She was too busy thinking about her favorite Thai restaurant to cure a hangover, which had been lost to her forever along the goddamned arrow of time.

"Sweet quasar!" Vel proclaimed, hopping down from her pod and stretching as soon as her boots hit the soft earth. "It's good to be here!"

Caid grinned suspiciously as he pretended to jump out of the pod as well. A close observer would've noticed his shoes disappearing halfway below the dirt before he recalibrated.

But there were no close observers around.

Captain Leviathan had the shine of determination in her eyes as she took in their surroundings and got a read on where the rendezvous point might be.

Vel had spent the last four and a half hours in therapy without realizing it.

Dan was feeling especially guilty about being the bearer of bad news for his captain.

And Alice was thinking about her favorite place on the Texas coast that was now undoubtedly under several feet of water. No one would ever smoke a spliff with a sunburned felon there again.

They'd landed on the moss-covered world of

Burfsdurfths (Bosks VFP34), full of green and purple growth. Large blooms emerged from the moss, opened wide, then closed and returned to their cover, like whales breaching the ocean's surface. What probably amounted biologically to trees looked more like clumps of cotton candy scattered about.

There was no sign of civilization in view.

"This way," said Captain Leviathan. "They should already be at the way station."

"You know these people?" Alice said, clumping along after, her hammies painfully tight from sitting.

"A few."

"But how? If they're on this planet a little too long, they could be dead by the time we reach them, right?" A mass of small flies crossed her path, and she waved them away and spat one out. Alien bugs. Nasty.

Captain Leviathan shot a questioning glance at Dan. "You explained it to her?"

"Only the basics."

"Right." She addressed Alice again. "It's complicated. Those of us living and working mostly off-planet have coordinated systems and communication methods that help avoid relativity problems in intergalactic travel."

"It's what my sister works on," said Dan, "with the Ministry of Communication and Sales."

"Ah yes," said Captain Leviathan. "It's hard to sell things to people without being able to communicate great distances and ensure the client isn't dead by the time the product is delivered."

"Why didn't anyone set up those systems with Earth, then?" Alice demanded. "I could still know living people from my planet."

"They did. At least partially," said Captain Leviathan. "The Depot headquarters is there, after all."

"But they could've—"

Captain Leviathan cut her off. "Does the Depot strike you as a corporation that wants competition?"

"Fair point," said Alice.

"Off-Earth, where everyone grows up knowing about time dilation, people have a choice to make. They can choose to live planet-bound or they can choose to live the traveler's life. Most people choose the former over the latter, and the universe ends up with two societies, essentially."

"Those who leave and those who get left?" said Alice.

Captain Leviathan inspected her thoughtfully. "I hadn't thought of it like that."

"Why would *anyone* choose to get left behind?" Alice asked.

"Why would anyone choose to leave it all behind?" Captain Leviathan countered.

Alice thought the answer to *that* was obvious.

But then again … she hadn't meant to leave *everything*. Only a few things. Or maybe just one thing.

"No one on Earth has been given the choice to stay or leave, though. Or only a few. No. Only me."

"And me," said Captain Leviathan. "I left."

Alice gasped, scandalized. "I thought you were from a parallel universe!"

"I am. This universe is parallel to many."

"And you and Susy?"

"We seem to be parallel versions of each other, wouldn't you say?"

"Either that or twins, but she swears up and down that

she—" Alice cut herself off when Vel made a slashing gesture across her throat.

"Not twins as far as I know," said Captain Leviathan. "I did have a twin, but she was evil, and I had to kill her."

"Really?" Vel's brows pinched together.

"No. Not really. That would be weird."

"Right," said Vel. "Super strange."

Alice couldn't help but look at Leviathan with new eyes now. Well, newer eyes. First, she had new eyes when the client turned out to be Alliance, and now she had newer eyes about the whole Earthling thing.

"Where are you from on Earth?"

"I'm Zapotec, and I was born on our lands in Oaxaca, Mexico. But I was always fascinated with space. I wanted to visit it, and my mother knew the only way that would be possible was if I moved to America, got an American education, and applied to NASA."

"So you *meant* to be an astronaut."

"Very much so. And I got it. I worked for NASA until the Depot recruited me."

"Did they act like an office supply store?" Alice asked. "I thought I was applying to an office supply store."

Captain Leviathan arched a brow at her. "No. I wouldn't have interviewed with an office supply store. I worked at NASA."

"Ah, right."

"What mission did they recruit you for?" Vel asked.

"Test mission one for the Depot. Nineteen eighty-seven. It was a success. We made it to space, visited another planet, arranged a match, then returned to Earth."

"Some success," muttered Vel. "You've turned against them."

"So have you. The Depot has a long history of success

turning to failure, but that's because they keep making the same mistake."

Dan hurried to catch up with the head of the group. "Then you must've known Caid prior to this."

"No," Caid answered. "I wasn't with the Depot that early. I was on the original mission, but not the test ones."

"I don't think I could've gotten this far undercover as a client if he'd recognized me." Leviathan peered ahead. "Through these trees."

She had to swat through the cotton candy barrier until it opened up and a structure appeared ahead. It was made of natural materials and covered by more of the violet and emerald moss.

Dan suspected it wouldn't be easy to spot with the naked eye from above, and that was probably intentional. After all, if this was one of the Alliance's spots, it was a nest of people with a bounty on their heads.

And Dan was about to walk straight into it.

The problem with outlaws, he'd found, wasn't that they were meaner or less good-hearted than anyone else. It was that they had less to lose. Bounties on your head could do that. If the authorities already wanted you dead, what were they going to do, want you deader? Outlaws could do as they pleased with no threat of increased retribution.

The wood door creaked in such a way that Dan wondered if the moss on top had been intentional or if this building was simply old and overgrown.

Beyond the door, the space was dim. A single room with a round table at the center awaited them, and around that table, lit only by what sunlight could penetrate the building's moss-covered windows, stood three figures.

Dan recognized two of them immediately.

So did Alice, but her attention went solely to one. "You!"

"Aw, come off it, you trigger-happy twat," the cactus said in his gravelly voice. "You're the one who shot my arm off, and I found a way to get over it, didn't I?"

The woman standing beside the cactus shot him a sharp look. "Lilqua'tartian, maybe now's not the time to call one of our guests a twat."

"Is that what we are?" Alice asked skeptically. "Guests?"

"This time, yes," replied Astra Blum.

Alice hadn't seen this Alliance leader since DeepService Team One's rescue mission of Vel. Blaster fire had been exchanged in that meeting, and Alice had obliterated Lilqua'tartian's arm. Not exactly great a peaceful parting.

But it was proving true that time could heal all things, including a cactus arm. Maybe even a rift like the one in the room at that very moment.

Shadow partly obscured Astra's face, but Alice had no trouble recalling the woman's appearance—her sable skin, the intensity behind her gray eyes, the weariness in the wrinkles around her lips. She was the kind of person Alice would normally want to impress, not shoot. "Perhaps you'll become allies once you know what we know," Astra added.

Alice massaged a crick in her neck that had taken root in the escape pod. "I think I already know enough to tell the Depot to fuck off. But that doesn't mean I trust any of y'all. Captain Leviathan seems alright, but—"

"President," said Astra quickly.

"Huh?"

"President Leviathan."

Never one to cling to reverence, Alice addressed Captain Leviathan with: "The fuck she talking about?"

"It's true."

"President of *what*?" Vel demanded.

"The Alliance."

"I thought it was a scattered thing," Dan said. "A bunch of factions."

"It was," said President Leviathan. "Turns out that's an ineffective way to run things. We needed someone at the center. They elected me."

"And you—" Something akin to admiration flooded Vel's face. "You infiltrated the Depot without them knowing you were not only Alliance, but the *president* of it?"

President Leviathan grinned. "Pretty good trick, huh?"

"I mean, *sure,*" Alice said begrudgingly. "It's pretty *cool.* It's a pretty *sexy* thing to do. I'm a little *turned on* by it. Sure. I think we all are. But we still need to know why you bothered saving us. You could've left on your own, taken an escape pod out."

"No, I couldn't have. When I tried to launch my pod, it didn't work. I tried everything. Only once I stopped trying did it grant me access."

"That was all Alice," Dan said proudly.

Alice felt another dagger through her heart. "No, it was Allura. She came through for us."

Caid appeared beside her, crooning, "Only because you treated her better than anyone ever had."

Alice attempted to shove him away, and he got the hint the third time her hands went through this chest and stepped back to give her space.

Dan cleared his throat. "The entire crew, but our

captain especially, has had a tough day. Can we get on with our business here?"

"Why don't we have a seat?" President Leviathan suggested.

"We're good," Dan said, planting his feet despite his insides feeling like jelly. "Who's that?" He nodded at the third figure, a full-figured Homo sapiens woman with amber skin and auburn hair, possibly the most beautiful being he'd ever laid eyes on.

"I'm Celeste," the figure replied.

"From Blerg VFP69?" Dan asked. "Or a parallel version?"

She smiled softly. "From the edge of the universe."

Alice snapped to attention. "Wait. Like, you're a hologram?"

"An organic hologram, yes."

"I'll be damned," Alice breathed. "Caid, have you met another hologram before? Caid?"

The crew aid was glaring at Celeste with malevolence Alice had never seen from the sensitive therapist, and Celeste was meeting that gaze unflinchingly.

The words were out of Alice's mouth before she could pull them back. "Oh shit, have y'all slept together?"

"That's not how it works," Caid muttered.

"But you know each other."

Celeste was the one to answer. "We've entangled before, yes. So good to see you, Caid Sonorian."

Alice held her hands in the air in surrender. "How in the *hell* is the universe this small?"

It was a fair question to ask. How the hell *is* the universe so small, especially when it's constantly expanding?

According to the Universal Law of Exes, any two

beings who have become quantum and/or emotionally entangled will later run into each other at least once in a space-time location where neither would likely be otherwise.

For Caid and Celeste, that was the planet of Burfsdurfths at $T=5671.93645283946001$ (with T being an unknown unit of time). It was among the least likely place in the universe that either of them should be, which was why they ran into each other there of all places.

Though Alice, like most Homo sapiens, was unaware of the Universal Law of Exes, she, like you, had experienced it in many forms and developed the appropriate dread when she left the house on those days where she put minimal effort into her appearance.

Fortunately for her, though, all her exes were now dead.

"Listen," said President Leviathan, "this is only meant to be a rendezvous point. There's a chance the Depot can still track their escape pods, despite the manual override, and we can't lead them to the main Alliance headquarters. We shouldn't stay here long. We'll transport you all safely off-planet, but first, we need your clothes."

Astra grabbed a sack at her feet and yanked open the drawstring, dumping a pile of linen out onto the table.

"The insignias," President Leviathan continued. "They send out a ping. It's supposed to be used as a distress signal, but I think we're past pretending the Depot cares about rescuing its own."

"These sons-a-bitches," Alice said, trying to yank off the offending patch on her chest and failing. "They really didn't trust us, did they?"

"Should they have?" Dan asked.

"True. Good call on their part."

Alice, Dan, and Vel rifled through the pile of clothes until they had what they needed. Most of the fabric was dyed in bland browns and creams, but Alice found a pair of powder-blue pants and snatched them to go with a cream blouse.

She did a quick change out of her jumpsuit in a dark corner of the room, stepping in and out of her cowboy boots as quickly as she could to keep her sock feet from getting chilly, and tossed the jumpsuit onto the table afterward.

"We'll get you more suitable clothes as soon as we can," President Leviathan said. "We'll leave soon. The transport is hidden out back. Before we get on it, though, I need you to know that I do not trust your word."

Dan and Vel shared an uneasy look.

"I have no reason to trust your word, do I? It's the same word you gave to the Depot, and now you're betraying them. The Alliance is full of traitors like you. I only trust deeds, and I only trust as far as our desired outcomes remain in accordance. The Alliance is important to me. It's all I care about. I like each of you, but if you betray us, I won't hold it against you, I will simply kill you myself."

"Christ," Alice said. "I'd hate to think what you'd do to people you don't like."

"Do we have an understanding on this?" asked President Leviathan.

Vel didn't appear fazed by the threat. "We do. I don't trust any of you, either, even though you're our lifeline, and I suspect we feel similarly about the Depot."

"No," President Leviathan said, smirking, "I assure you that we do *not* feel the same about the Depot. Maybe once you know more, but not yet. My hatred for them lives in the atoms of my body. Yours is hardly skin deep yet." She turned to Astra Blum, who slung the bag of unused clothes over her shoulder and nodded for them to follow her out the back door of the building. The former DeepService Team One stuck closely together, keeping distance from the Alliance members for all the obvious reasons.

"We got a saying for this back on—" Alice remembered again. "We *had* a saying for this back on Earth. Out of the frying pan and into the fire."

"I think I understand what that means," Dan muttered. "And perhaps there are still people there saying it. You never know."

Alice rolled her eyes, because certainty that everyone was dead was somehow much lighter to carry than uncertainty about it, so she'd take the certainty, please!

"It's not much," said President Leviathan farther down the path, "but the ship can accommodate up to fifteen people, so we shouldn't be stepping on each other's toes."

Dan had to squint to find the first glimmer of metal beneath the moss blanket, and it wasn't much of a glimmer. The ship looked nearly rusted out.

As the Alliance members set to uncovering the craft, easily the size of half a football field, Vel leaned in toward Dan. "At least if we're all on the same ship, we know they won't fly us into the nearest black hole."

Dan inspected her. "How are you able to do this? Just carry on without stressing? They've already kidnapped you once, and now you trust them?"

"I already said I don't," she corrected him. "I trust *me*. And I trust *us*." She patted him on the back, then jogged over to help them finish prepping the craft, which was taking way too long, in her opinion.

Alice hated this new ship from the moment she stepped on and heard the operating system speak.

"Welcome, President Leviathan. Your presence is a true honor."

"Suck-up," Alice muttered, following the Alliance members into the loading dock and toward a set of stairs leading to the upper deck. The damn thing wasn't even ADA compliant. Hunk of crap.

Vel leaned closer to Dan. "What's her problem?" She motioned to Alice. "She's not her usual dangerously enthusiastic self."

"Of course not. She found out everyone she ever knew is most likely dead."

Vel arched an eyebrow. "Most likely? You mean definitely. And why is that such a big deal?"

"You weren't sad when you left your planet behind?"

"I left my whole *universe* behind. But it didn't matter. I was fighting for too long. I knew what that meant about the people I'd left behind while I was zipping around from battlefield to battlefield. I was more concerned with the people dying right next to me. They were the ones who chose to come with me, to join the fight. I don't care about the people who want to stay home and live their quiet little lives. I hope they enjoyed them while they lasted."

"You knew, though," Dan said. "You knew it was happening. Alice just found out. She's in shock, and it's not the best time for processing, I don't think. I have less of an idea about what she'll do next than I usually do. We ought to keep an eye on her."

"I always do," Vel replied. "That's why we're still alive."

CHAPTER
TWELVE

The former crew of DeepService Team One were situated at the back of the Alliance ship's upper deck on a viewing platform made for relaxing and gazing at the cosmos.

They weren't relaxed, but they *did* gaze at the cosmos.

I mean, come on. It's the *cosmos*. It's fucking awesome.

Quark Leviathan, as it turned out, had never even been to Del'evvia, nor did she represent the Fnori people. It was all a lie, but airtight enough that the Depot had fallen for it.

The liar remained on the bridge of the ship with Astra Blum, Lilqua'tartian, and Celeste, while the others recovered on the observation deck, and the mutual mistrust between groups served both just fine.

Alice and Caid rested in a pair of padded, reclining chairs with a small wet bar on Alice's other side. There was nothing in it; she'd checked immediately.

"Your vibration," Caid said, breaking what Alice considered a welcome silence. "It's sluggish. You're taking this hard."

"So hard," Alice said wistfully, missing Allura more than ever.

"You're in a grieving process, and that's understandable."

"I'm not grieving. I'm pissed off."

"Huh?"

She gripped the ends of the padded armrests, digging her nails into the material. "I'm fucking pissed! I feel like I could destroy something. I *want* to destroy something. Then I want to run away. Then I want to destroy something else."

"And whose stuff do you want to destroy?" asked Caid.

Not surprisingly, she hadn't thought that far. But now she did. "The universe's. Anything the universe holds dear, I want to ruin it."

"Hmm," Caid crooned thoughtfully. "What if I told you the universe holds nothing dear?"

Alice laughed dryly. "That would make sense. It doesn't take good care of its things."

She expected the hologram to offer some defense of the universe, but instead, he said, "True. Entropy's a bitch."

After a moment's silence, where Alice struggled with whether she should ask what entropy was, she decided instead to change the subject. "I'm homeless, Caid."

He slipped his hands behind his head. "You had a home on Blerg VFP69?"

"Of course I … Technically I lived with …" But she could muster no oomph behind it.

"If I remember correctly from our talks, you ran away from your so-called home many times growing up until you were finally kicked out. When you lived with your boyfriend, you always felt like it was *his* home. Then you hopped on a spacecraft and left that behind, too. What home are you going without, exactly?"

"I had this apartment," she said, "my third senior year of college. I had three roommates—Britta, Jenn, and Rochelle. We lived together for two full years before they moved away. That was home."

"And what about that felt like home?"

Alice shook her head. She was exhausted. "I don't know. Does it even matter? They're all dead now. I wonder how they died. Maybe cancer? Hit by a bus? Abused by their nursing home staff?"

Caid tilted his head, gazing softly at her. "I hope you can find home again."

"Nah. I don't reckon it's in the cards for me. I mean, look around us! We're floating out in space, and the only people who know where we are are on this ship. I'll likely die out here before I get the chance to settle down. But hey, it beats breast cancer."

"Does it?"

From the set of chairs a few feet away, Dan said, "What do you think, Alice?"

"'Bout what?" she barked.

"She's holding a lot of interesting thoughts right now," Caid explained.

Dan clarified. "You think we're the good guys?"

Alice grunted. "Hell if I know."

"See?" Vel said. "Nobody cares, Dan."

"I care," Caid said. "I care an awful lot."

"Ya know what?" Alice said, staring out the window again. "I reckon it doesn't matter if we're good or bad. Not out here in the middle of a universe that doesn't have two fucks to rub together about us."

"That's an interesting take," Caid mused. "Would you be interested in exploring that more?"

"Why not?" she said. "Ain't got shit else to do." She tucked her hands behind her head, crossed her ankles, and started in. "Y'all gotta understand that I was raised with a whole lotta Jesus. I remember hearing in elementary school that the most commonly used letter was E, and all I could think was, *That can't be right. It's gotta be S because there's only one E in Jesus and two esses.* Every other word outta some folks' mouths was that goddamn name. You can't help but have it seep into your bones when you grow up in Texas, whether the story makes any sense to you or not. Hell, even the Jews celebrate Christmas where I'm from. It's not religion, it's a way of life. Christian is a language you speak. It's the way your thoughts form themselves.

"But I'm starting to think none of that matters out here. Church was all about 'joy to the world' and 'on Earth as it is in Heaven.' There's not a single mention of Jesus giving a holy flying fuck what happens in outer space." She sighed, watching the stars float by in the distance. "Begs the question: if you sin in outer space and no Christians are around to judge you, is it really a sin?" She looked at the others ... who had nothing for her.

"Remind me," said Dan, "was Jesus the guy on the TV show?"

"Nooo," Alice replied, serving him up serious side-eye. "But now I need to know who the hell you think Jesus was. What TV show?"

"Where they compete to survive."

"*Survivor?*"

"Yes! Universally beloved. Syndicated just about

everywhere. Humans are incredibly messy things. Jesus was the host of it, yes?"

Alice sucked on her teeth. "You think Jesus was Jeff Probst." She felt something solid inside her chest crack. "I reckon that about answers my philosophical quandary. No, Dan, I don't think we're the good guys. But we're not the bad guys either. We're just … guys. Guys in space."

Caid cleared his throat. "Morality still exists in—"

"Shhh," she said as she closed her eyes and leaned her head back. "Don't ruin the vibe."

Though nobody was aware or frankly *cared* to be aware of it, Dan Zone had the best eyesight of the entire former DeepService Team One. Not only would it have been labeled 20/5 by an ophthalmologist, but his eyes saw a broader spectrum of visible light, had stronger night vision, and were more sensitive to movement than those of Alice and Vel.

Caid, meanwhile, didn't technically *see* anything in the strict sense of the word. His vision ran on vibes.

The reason no one was ever aware that Dan had better vision was because no one ever looked into it, but also because Dan was usually so lost in his head, worrying about possible future dangers, that he was sometimes the last to notice the present ones.

However, this time, he was the first to see what was fast approaching the Alliance transit: crimson and azure flashing lights.

To see something flashing red and blue, colors at opposite ends of the visible spectrum, is a universally alarming thing. Nothing should be flashing blue *and* red.

In terms of the universe, which most things are, that pairing of lights sends a primal signal that something is rapidly moving toward then away then toward then away again, and that's never a good sign. It's like Blerg VFP69 chimps showing their teeth or Blerg VFP69 humans saying, "No one will even notice."

Also, it's the po-po.

"Void," cursed Dan.

Vel sat up straight. "What?"

"Out there. The lights."

Vel spotted them next. "Oh, wow. How did you see those so far away?"

"What are those?" Alice asked. "Who is that?"

"Universal enforcement. Patrollers," said Vel. "We should probably hide."

The hair stood up on Alice's arms at the warrior's suggestion of retreat. "Cool, let's do that."

They scurried off the observation deck and onto the bridge, where the Alliance members were already scrambling.

President Leviathan glanced over her shoulder as they entered. "Get out of here. You're wanted people."

"If we are, then you are, too," Alice said.

Astra Blum had a deep crease in her forehead as she manipulated the controls. "Only one patrol craft. No word from them yet. I got it from here if you need to take cover, President."

No sooner had she spoken than a call came through from the dashboard. She waved the fugitives out of sight.

President Leviathan led them into a hallway, then paused, turning an ear toward the bridge as she held a finger to her lips.

Astra Blum answered the call.

"Greetings," came a gurgling voice. "This is Patrollers Greeps and Athlathglath'n. We've gotten word that a ship in this star system might be harboring Depot fugitives. We need you to open your dock to us for an all-ship inspection."

"I can assure you we're not harboring any fugitives," said Astra Blum.

"Noted. We will still have to conduct our search anyway. Please, may we have your name?"

"Agnola Gff. And these are my assistants, Callt Gnoman and Spirulyndactir."

"Please state your business."

"Carrier ship. We're subcontractors with the Ministry of Communication and Sales."

"Noted. Do you have any weapons onboard?"

"Yes, of course. Three ATK Mag 34 blasters, and a plutonium ray cannon."

"Noted. That's all?"

"Yes, Patroller."

"Noted. Please leave all weapons at the entrance of the dock for us to inspect, and then we will meet you on the bridge."

Astra Blum, cursing under her breath, signaled to the eavesdropping others that the call had ended. "Lilqua'tartian? Would you move the weapons as asked?"

"You know I hate the name Callt Gnoman," muttered the cactus.

"Ask me if I care," Astra Blum replied, glaring at him with her fists on her hips. "It's the only fake credentials we could get for a void-sucked cactus."

"I quite like Spirulyndactir," Celeste said dreamily. "It's seductive in its own way."

Lilqua'tartian passed the hallway where the rest were

hiding and snapped, "You can come out. It'll be a minute before they can dock." Then he disappeared down the stairs to the lower deck to prepare the weapons as requested.

President Leviathan stepped out of the hiding spot. "What's your assessment, Astra?"

"Patroller Greeps is a Bacc'joon, so no concerns there. But I caught a glimpse of Patroller Athlathglath'n, and he seemed to be a splatterpoot."

"A splatterpoot?" Vel demanded. "A male splatterpoot?"

"Hold on," said Dan. "Did you say Patroller Greeps was a Bacc'joon?"

It clicked with Vel as soon as she heard it repeated, and her brows shot up.

"Yes," Astra replied. "A new race out of Bacc'nalia and Location." Her gaze held a stark accusation in it, and not without reason.

"Wait!" Alice spat. "You mean it's one of *ours*?"

Astra pressed her lips together into a thin line. "Maybe wait to meet one before you well up with pride."

Alice looked around at the others. "Is this a time dilation thing? Is that why there are already adult ones running around?" Dan nodded. "Awww, they're playing cops, too!"

"Which means now isn't the best time to meet your creation," added President Leviathan. "Astra, Lilqua'tartian, and Celeste have fake identities, but I have a feeling these patrollers will be bringing images of the wanted fugitives. The rest of us need to hide."

Astra handed a palm-sized tablet to the president. "So you can know if they're coming your way."

On tiptoes, Alice peered over the president's shoulder

and saw … herself on the screen. Well, the top of her head as she gazed down at the screen. She looked up. "Where is it?"

Astra pointed to a button on her vest.

Fist-pumping the air, Alice counted down the moments until she'd see her first Bacc'joon through Astra's hidden camera.

President Leviathan led them out of the bridge, down a narrow and dim hallway, past a series of doors, and stopped at what looked like a flat wall. She pressed her hand to it, and it slid open from the floor. Behind it, a series of pipes and gears. "We'll have to squeeze in. Don't touch that"—she pointed to a white-hot pipe—"if you want to keep your skin on you."

They slid in, shoulder to shoulder, each person's nose nearly pressing against the interior of the hallway wall.

Alice made sure to slide in next to the president so she could see the tablet screen.

On the screen, Lilqua'tartian appeared back on the bridge, and those behind the wall waited not-so-patiently as the minutes passed.

The sound of footsteps on the stairs up to the bridge could only have been from Patroller Greeps, since Patroller Athlathglath'n, a male splatterpoot, had no feet.

The latter appeared on the screen first, and Alice cringed. Her mind, in all its self-preserving glory, had glossed over just how disgusting male splatterpoots were. But catching sight of this one brought back all those repressed memories of the president of Texas, his acidic slime trail, and those weird tentacle suckers.

But whereas the president of Texas wore a crown, Patroller Athlathglath'n wore a small black cap with a gold star in the center. Not a five-pointed star; a big, glowing ball. She thought she saw a flare erupt quickly from it.

Always one for shiny objects, Alice was so entranced by the hat that she didn't notice the next guy right away. Then suddenly there he was, her indirect creation.

A Bacc'joon.

"Ewww," she said. "*No bueno.*"

It was beyond *no bueno,* however. The Bacc'joon was, in fact, *horribilísimo.* It was *monstruoso.*

"That looks *nothing* like the simulation I ran," she muttered in her own defense.

"Almost like the Depot lied to you," Vel replied from President Leviathan's other side. What she didn't add was: *Almost like they hired someone they could easily lie to.*

The Bacc'joon had the following notable features:

A Bacc'nali head with a smaller head growing from the top of it. (The smaller head was the one wearing the patroller hat.)

A squished marshmallow middle with no neck separating it from the double-decker heads.

Two nubby legs.

One Bacc'nalian "third leg" that escaped from the left pant cuff and dragged on the floor behind the rest of him.

"It's a boy," Alice said, grimacing.

Dan pressed the side of his face against the wall to see the screen. "That can't be sanitary."

"Congratulations due all around," President Leviathan said dryly. "A successful Depot mission if ever there was one."

Alice swallowed down a bit of bile as the Bacc'joon's unwieldy penis caught on a table leg as he passed it. "To be fair, it was only a trial. Are they *all* like that?"

"No," said President Leviathan. "Most are worse." She

brought her finger to her lips and turned her attention back to the screen, where the patrollers were telling Astra, Lilqua'tartian, and Celeste to stay put and not try any funny business during the search.

"I'm afraid I must insist on accompanying you," said Astra. "Some of the equipment we're carrying is highly protected, and I could lose my contract with the Ministry of Communication and Sales if I let anyone around it unsupervised."

"We're patrollers!" shouted Athlathglath'n, his jowls quivering. "We have authority!"

"Not unlimited authority." Astra took a bold step toward the splatterpoot, which seemed ill-advised to all those watching behind the wall.

"We work for the government!"

"That's one way to pronounce 'Depot.'"

"How dare you!" A small squirt of goo ejected from beneath him; Lilqua'tartian hopped out of the way. The goo sizzled where it landed. "We can't be bought!"

"Easy, friend." Astra took a step back. "I'm giving you a hard time. I know you have a job to do. You need to check for a fugitive."

"Fugitives," he corrected her. "Five of them."

Patroller Greeps reached for something in his pants pocket. Unfortunately, it was the one on his right side, which was absolutely snug due to the extra object filling the left pant leg. He struggled, then eventually produced a small metallic ball. A holographic projection appeared above, and in that projection, those hiding behind the wall saw their own faces.

"The hell?" Alice whispered. "That's my college ID photo. I was a baby in that thing."

"You sound offended when you should sound relieved," Dan replied. "Makes you harder to spot."

"If they can't deduce it's me by the fact that I'm hanging out with y'all, then that's their bad."

President Leviathan nudged her to shut the hell up.

On the screen and back on the bridge, Astra shrugged. "Nah, never seen them. You can search, of course, but I do need to accompany you, like I said."

"She seems nice," said the Bacc'joon, one of his eyes rolling outward while the other remained focused on Astra. "I'd like to lick her."

"Not now," snapped the splatterpoot. "But maybe later."

Astra maintained a poker face Alice didn't know was possible in such a situation, and said, "Lead the way, patrollers."

A full tour of the ship followed, with Patroller Athlathglath'n pausing on the observation deck to stare at the chair Alice had occupied not even a quarter of an hour before. Did he see something there? Had she left a trace without meaning to?

But then he blinked with a distinct slurping sound and slugged away.

The patrollers walked right past the hiding spot the first time. President Leviathan had muted the tablet, and everyone, even Caid, held their breath.

The individual living quarters, the meeting rooms, the exercise room, the laundry room, the mess hall, the byglametry room, which was something that confused Alice as to its purpose but made sense to anyone who'd met a Flocktuh from Gorlglathla, which most beings in the universe had—all were searched thoroughly before the patrollers felt confident enough to head back out again.

And when they did, as they approached the hiding place in the wall, Patroller Athlathglath'n paused and gurgled. "Sweet *void*, what is that awful smell?"

Alice exchanged a glance with Dan. He frowned and shook his head.

"It smells like *Homo sapiens!* I always know that putrescence when I smell it."

Alice puffed up her chest, indignant. Vel reached across President Leviathan to slap a hand over her captain's mouth, muffling Alice's predictable protestations.

"Excuse me?" Astra said. "What are you implying? That we would let a *Homo sapiens* on this ship?"

Patroller Athlathglath'n looked her up and down. "No, I suppose you aren't quite Homo sapiens yourself. At least you don't smell like one."

"That's because I'm not. I'm from the universe Pallora, connected by the B47 wormhole."

"And do your people smell putrescent?"

"No. That's one of the differences."

"But it definitely smells like a Homo sapiens from Blerg VFP69, right, Greeps?"

Greeps inhaled deeply, his lolling penis contracting slightly with the effort. "Maybe? It's hard to tell. I wasn't born with a strong sense of smell."

"You have other gifts," Patroller Athlathglath'n assured him. "No, I'm *sure* I smell a Homo sapiens. But where?"

Those in hiding braced as the splatterpoot's tentacle ran over the wall not three feet from where they were.

Then Alice heard a pop beside her.

"What's that sound?" demanded Athlathglath'n.

"I didn't hear anything," Astra said.

"I definitely heard something!"

"Me too," said Greeps. "My hearing is good. Second only to my penis."

Patroller Athlathglath'n groaned. "Can we respond to a *single* call without you mentioning it?"

"I can't help it."

"That's obvious enough. I'd tell you to keep it in your pants, but—" The rest of the words caught in his jowls.

"Who the fuck?" Alice whispered. She shouldn't've whispered with the patrollers so close, but thankfully they were distracted. When no one answered, she looked to Caid … who was no longer there. "Oh my God."

"Hey, boys." A busty blonde with bedroom eyes and hips you could set a pint glass on without spilling it strolled down the hall toward Astra and the patrollers, eyeing each of the males up and down with an impish grin. "My, oh, my."

Astra opened her mouth but seemed at a loss of words.

But because Caid had no idea who Mae West was, as is probably the case for most people reading this, he didn't know to call himself by that name.

However, he'd started to recognize the feeling of change that accompanied the small popping and knew that he was definitely *not* Caid. And judging by the lecherous looks he was getting from all three of those staring at him, he thought only a universally feminine name would suffice, since people gawked at sexy women similarly throughout the multiverse, despite the protestations of said sexy women, who were, after all, weird biological specimens with sentience who were unlucky enough to be rated as tens.

"I'm Hank," said Caid.

With few exceptions, Hank was considered a stereotypically sexy female name.

It could've been Caid's undoing—a sexy woman named Hank was a little *too* clichéd—but the thing about sexy women is that they lower the IQ in whatever closed space they enter, the only exception being the vacuum of space, where the IQ becomes irrelevant unless you're a tardigrade who can survive it.

"Hello, Hank," said Patroller Athlathglath'n, apparently dropping his contempt for Homo sapiens instantly. "My name is Pis. I have a lot of authority."

Caid giggled. "How'd you know I like that?"

"You do?" A squelching announced a fresh slime ejection, and the floor beneath Athlathglath'n smoldered.

"Depends," Caid replied. "Are you gonna use it on me?"

"You want me to?"

"Only if you know how." Caid winked at the patroller.

Alice found her heart aching one again. *Allura would love this.*

Caid smoothed his hands down his curves. "You know what I really love?"

"What?" said Athlathglath'n and Greeps together.

"I love a man in authority who's *bad*."

(A single tear ran down Alice's cheek.)

"Bad?" said Greeps. "As in one that'll lick you when you didn't ask for it?"

Athlathglath'n shot him a fierce look. "We've been over this. No licking."

"No," said Caid. "Not *that* kind of bad."

"What about one with a big, useless penis?" Greeps asked, wetting his lips.

Alice barely stifled a gag.

Caid himself faltered, his gaze jumping quickly to the thing hanging from Greeps' pants. His expression was about as far from enticed as possible. "That's, uh, that's not nothing. But what I like is a man with authority who breaks the rules."

"So you *do* want me to lick you."

Athlathglath'n smacked his partner in the chest. "Not what this fine lady is saying."

"It would absolutely set my furnace ablaze if you cut this search short. Maybe take me back to your ship?"

The patrollers were silent for a moment, then Athlathglath'n turned to Astra and said, "Thank you for your compliance in this search. We'll be taking off now with your crew member Hank."

Astra glanced at Caid, who consented with a subtle nod. "Okay, then. Fine. Right this way."

Alice watched the group saunter off, Caid keeping his distance from the patrollers so one could get a big idea about trying to touch him and realize who and what they were dealing with.

Once the tablet screen showed the group descend into the loading dock of the ship, President Leviathan indicated they were safe to leave their hiding place.

"Chrissake," Alice muttered, stretching out her neck. "Now we gotta go rescue Caid from their ship." She grunted. "If y'all could stop getting kidnapped, that'd be great." She tried to glare at Vel, but the lieutenant's look of scorn stopped her. "What?"

"You know Caid doesn't have to breathe, right?"

"So?"

"And he can move through walls."

"Wait," Alice said, holding up her hand. "Are you telling me he's a ghost?"

"No."

"Because it sounds like you're describing a ghost."

"He's a holo— Do you really believe you've been hanging out with a ghost?"

Dan wiped some dust from his shirt. "He does have ghostly qualities."

Alice pointed at him. "See? It's not just me."

"He's decidedly a hologram, though," Dan added.

"Traitor."

"What? I thought you already knew that! It's been explained to you! You've experienced it. He's an organic—"

"My point," Vel said, cutting back in, "is that he can get on that ship with them and then rescue himself. We need to be ready."

President Leviathan led the way back onto the bridge to do just that.

When Lilqua'tartian, Celeste, and Astra returned, Leviathan said, "He left with them?"

"He did." Astra met the president at the controls. "We're to hold steady here until he arrives, then we need to hit it."

"Already amassing propulsion energy," confirmed Leviathan.

"Where are we going?" Alice asked.

"The Assembly."

They all watched as the enforcement vehicle came into view after undocking and slowly floating away.

"He *will* be able to escape, right?" Alice asked, wondering, not for the first time, how ghosts got on in space.

Celeste was the one to answer. "His form will escape easily enough. But depending on what they try on that ship, a piece of his heart might be left behind."

"At least we know we have a replacement Caid if something goes wrong," Alice muttered.

But nothing went wrong. At least not physically, and not counting the Bacc'joon monstrosity that had already gone very, very wrong in its very creation.

A few minutes later, Alice saw the tiny glow appear outside the patrollers' craft. It grew as it came closer, closer, and appeared to be slightly undulating.

No, not undulating, swimming. A breaststroke.

Caid looked like his old self again as he passed through the viewing window and landed gracefully on the bridge in front of his captain.

Alice opened her mouth to ask him where they'd touched him, but before she could, Astra said. "Hold on. We're hitting it to the nearest space fold." Then bam, the stars blurred, and they were outta there.

CHAPTER
THIRTEEN

Vel's hackles rose as their ship lowered toward the perfectly civilized planet of Famzonn. It was night on their hemisphere, and clusters of lights speckled the globe, islands of them connected by glowing arteries. When one zoomed out, every universe took on a similar pattern of light made up of stars and galaxies, and Vel understood that each planet was a universe unto itself.

Did civilizations muddy the waters by exporting their culture to other planets? Sure. That was Dan's whole job, whether he'd admit it or not. But just because there were connections between planets didn't mean the planets themselves would blur into one purely monolithic culture.

There were also connections between universes, natural highways that had formed long, long ago, allowing the dimensions to mix, swirl, and settle into the configuration she now enjoyed and that allowed travel from one parallel universe to the other without catastrophic dimensional snafus, but even *that* didn't mean each universe wasn't its own entity within the greater multiverse. Things were all the same—all part of the bigger whole, sure, but they were still individual, still separate.

Was homogeny peace? The Depot sure seemed to think so. Vel wasn't so sure. Sometimes homogeny was tyrannical. In fact, in her experience, it always was. Homogeny naturally arose nowhere. Nature always opted for diversity, for options.

Those she'd met in the Alliance seemed to understand that much, but by no means did that mean she trusted them yet.

And the fact that they were about to land on a planet that appeared to have advanced tech when five of them were wanted fugitives spoke of recklessness so severe it nudged up against malevolence.

But while she saw almost every feature of herself reflected back in Quark Leviathan, she didn't see a shared concern.

Instead, Lev busied herself in the landing procedures. "Sending word to the hangar. Hangar 74 confirms space. Manifest sent ahead."

"Who's working the traffic there?" Astra asked, working the manual controls.

"HKarrk. She's one of mine. She'll confirm the manifest once we disembark."

"Security?"

"A few cameras," Leviathan replied. "But they have a tendency to cut out."

"Amazing how that works."

Alice sidled up to Dan. "You think they have any pizza on this planet?"

"Something like it, probably. Most places do. Yeasted bread, acidic fruit sauce, and processed dairy product create a flavor combination millions of civilizations around the universe have evolved a preference for. No colonization necessary. It keeps popping up, and usually early on in a civilization's history."

"Like tacos?"

"Like tacos. Flattened grains, starch, processed dairy product, protein, and something punishingly spicy—those are the staples. Arranged in a variety of ways, sure, but the same basic ingredients."

"You also described Mexican food as a whole."

"Did I?" Dan looked delighted.

Turning her attention to the viewing window, Alice whistled at the approaching planet below. "If this place has pizza and tacos, I'm faking my death and settling down."

"Maybe you should get the feel of it first," Dan said, not believing she would actually do it, but also not *not* believing she would actually do it. It was best, he'd found, to assume anything was possible, and with entropy being what it was, things fell apart, crews included.

It was the first time that Dan had considered that this might be the beginning of the end for these friendships, if he dared call them that. He certainly considered Alice, Vel, and Caid his friends. They were his only friends, come to think of it. Hopping time folds had a way of doing that, of narrowing the friend pool dramatically.

The thought of *any* of the crew, let alone Alice, who, while making him perpetually nervous, seemed to appreciate him more than anyone else, left him with a feeling not unlike the onset of the jitters.

But it wasn't that. He was intimately familiar with *this* feeling. It was his shadow, his bedfellow, old reliable: it was fear. Good old fear. Wherever he went, it would go. He had to appreciate its undying loyalty, if nothing else.

Or maybe he was the one loyal to it?

By the time those aboard the ship were stepping out into the dusty hangar, Dan's fear had enough stimulation from the novel environment to only indirectly bug him through his subconscious. His conscious mind, meanwhile, was happily preoccupied with the crush of sound from the nearby marketplace. There was some relative safety in the anonymity one found in a crowd, but more than that, he'd never been to this planet before, so there was a whole new world of not only culture, but also weapons for him to learn about.

"Ghaat'll VFP9001," President Leviathan said over her shoulder as they followed her toward the edge of the market. "Also known as Vongarian."

"Never heard of it," said Dan, raising his voice to be heard above the noise.

"It's mostly a trading planet. Essentially a mall. The native inhabitants were smart enough to give up a third of the planet entirely for development right off the bat, consolidating all their people and weapons into a smaller terrain to defend. They signed a whole heap of treaties and agreements and then moved on."

"A third of the planet is for shopping?" Dan asked.

"Almost. There are still parts of that section that haven't been developed yet. But they will be. Most planets try to fight commercial development the whole way and lose bit by bit, ending up with far less than two-thirds of the planet healthy and untouched by consumerism. The Vongaars were wise to approach it that way. Huge loss of vegetative and animal life, of course. You can't carve out a chunk out of a planetary ecosystem and expect it to be okay right off. But the planet is slowly course-correcting.

Unpredictable weather in the meantime, hence the way they set up the markets."

The market they were fast approaching had tall stone walls jutting up on either side of the rows of kiosks and seller's tables. But while it was mostly open-air, a thick canopy that Dan assumed to be waterproof hung above, connecting to the tops of the stone barriers. Rain, wind, perhaps even a hurricane wouldn't stop the shopping.

A sign greeted them at the edge that read:

NO splatterpoots

NO haggling

NO exposed acidic skin

Of all the bans, the haggling one left Dan the most surprised. Haggling was an essential part of the marketplace experience as he knew it.

"No ban on glochids," remarked Lilqua'tartian, running the end of his arm over the spines of the other. "I'm good to go."

Passing between the two stone walls felt like entering a labyrinth. The chaos was immediate, with beings of all physical compositions pushing and shoving to get to where they needed to go. Unsurprisingly, the crowd parted slightly to allow Lilqua'tartian through.

Lots of those among the throng were yelling, though Dan suspected that was less out of anger and more a culturally accepted way to speak. He tried to ask Leviathan, "Why no haggling?" but his words were drowned out, and he decided there would be time for questions later.

Alice, meanwhile, was overstimulated, which she still considered under-stimulated. She felt something slimy brush against her hand and turned to see a glistening starfish-looking guy hopping in the other direction. "Neat," she muttered, though nobody heard.

While President Leviathan had said this was essentially a mall, it didn't look like the malls Alice had gone to as a kid. Slip'n'Fall, Texas didn't have its own mall, so she and her rotating cast of high school friends would drive fifty minutes to the nearest one to walk around, eat soft pretzels, try on clothes their parents would whoop them for wearing, laugh too loudly in the gag gift stores, and occasionally shoplift jewelry that turned their skin green in less than a week.

This was not like that. Where were the pretzels? The orange chicken? The gag gifts?

Then she saw it.

At a small kiosk, a being with a Buddha belly, one large eye, and elephant ears was bracing itself while a fishlike seller shoved a large hoop through said ear. A piercing pagoda! "This place rocks!"

Vel leaned in. "What?"

"This place rocks!" Alice repeated, just as enthusiastically.

Vel inspected her. "You know we're not here to shop, correct?"

"Who goes to a mall to *shop*? That's not the point at all."

"Maybe we should stay focused on the upcoming assembly, Captain."

Alice perked up. "Hey! We're not Depot anymore, remember? That means I'm not your captain and you're not my lieutenant. We're just a couple a best friends on a space adventure together!"

But while the idea lifted considerable weight from Alice's shoulders, it felt oppressive to Vel. Not only had the comfort of a clear chain of command and hierarchy been lost, but Alice might be right. No matter how much Vel tried to deny it, Alice, Dan, and Caid *might* be her best friends.

Vel couldn't help but re-evaluate her major life decisions, trying to pinpoint where things had gotten so off track.

Dan wasn't a bad friend to have. He was cautious, informed, diplomatic, and dangerous when backed into a corner. And Caid …

She shifted her attention his way, where he was saying, "Sorry. Pardon me. Excuse me. Pardon me …" to every matter-abled being he passed through.

She supposed Caid was a useful friend. He had perspective, you could generally trust him with your secrets (the Depot breach aside), he never said anything hurtful, and he genuinely cared about the safety and emotional well-being of those around him.

And then there was Alice, who—

Vel looked around.

Where had Alice gone?

"SUSY!"

Vel tracked the voice to find Alice at a booth a few yards back. "Sweet void," Vel muttered as she backtracked. "Did you have to do that *now*?"

Alice sat on the tall stool of the piercing pagoda, crinkling her nose, tears streaming down her face. "I've always wanted to do it."

Vel cursed to herself a few more times. "But did you have to do it *now*?"

"How does it look?" Alice tilted her head so Vel could see the glimmering green jewel at the end of the nostril piercing. "Is it cute?"

"Sure." Vel waved down the others, who had begun to realize they'd lost numbers.

The fishlike piercer handed over a mirror, and Alice admired her new addition while the seller explained in garbled English how to use the care package it would send home with her.

"Great, great," she said, not listening at all.

When she began to pay, offering up her eye for a biometric scan that would link to her overfull bank credits, Vel grabbed her by the shoulder and yanked her back. "Are you stupid?"

"Whoa, whoa, whoa. I didn't go to college for eight years to be called stupid."

"You almost gave up your location to the Depot."

"Oh."

Vel waved over Astra and explained the situation while Alice smartly kept her mouth shut.

Astra seemed confused, and rightfully so, but handed over a flat, round piece of metal that the fish dude ran under a green scanner, then said, "We'll have to get you set up with untraceable payment. Unfortunately, that means none of the money in your Depot account will be accessible until we can find a transfer kiosk somewhere in the middle of nowhere. We make the transfer out of the Depot account, transfer it a few more times through untraceable accounts, then hop on the nearest space fold and get to the other side of the universe before Depot ships can arrive to track us. It's a pain in the ass, but it keeps you alive."

"Good thinking," said Alice.

She ran a finger over her piercing, but Vel yanked her hand away. "You're inviting infection."

When they caught up to the others, Dan said, "Where did you— Ooh! Nice. Love that color for you."

"Thanks, Dan," Alice replied. "You're so supportive of my dreams." She shot Vel a harsh look that the woman missed entirely.

"This way," President Leviathan said, leading them off the main avenue and into one of the few indoor areas. This one was a restaurant, and the scent of roasted meats greeted them the second they stepped out of the bustle and into the quieter space.

While the tables were almost entirely full, they were spread out, so each one had a little breathing room. Leviathan nodded to the woman behind the counter, who then motioned with one of her flippers for another employee to scoot two tables together for their new guests.

"Be with you in a second, Lev," squeaked the beflippered woman.

Alice, who was always ready to chow down on some grub, was surprised they'd stopped in. She'd expected this trip to be all business. "Do they have tacos?"

Leviathan grinned. "Oh yeah. The best."

"That's not why we're here, though, right?" asked Vel. "We didn't come in for the tacos."

Leviathan almost grinned. "Not entirely, but partially, yes. I'm here for the tacos."

As the woman with the flippers stepped out from behind the counter, it was revealed that she had two perfectly normal legs.

Dan knew better than to overthink why evolution would work in such a way. For most beings he'd met, evolution did whatever seemed right at the time, and there wasn't much more that went into it.

It must've been very strange times indeed whenever this woman's species evolved. Her flippers were surprisingly dexterous, unlikely to be vestigial, and she used them to carry a tray of clay mugs out to the table, where she passed them out to each of her guests. Outside of that particular anomaly, she looked mostly humanoid with green-gray skin. "Welcome back, Lev. Always good to see you. Lilqua'tartian, Astra, Celeste." She offered a friendly smile with each name. Then her attention fell on Vel. "Is this your sister, Lev?"

"Yes," the Alliance president lied. "She's come to visit."

"Wonderful! You should take her to the Guarly Dungeons after this."

"Is that the place a block north of Boson and Up Quark?"

"You got it." The woman proceeded to hand out menus, then left to check on another table.

"What's with the no-haggling rule?" Dan could finally ask.

"Vendors gotta get all prices preapproved," Lilqua'tartian said bitterly. He chugged down the liquid in his mug and slammed it back on the table.

"Preapproved by who?" Dan asked.

"Who do you think?" the cactus snapped.

Dan looked from Leviathan to Astra to Celeste, his mouth slowly falling open. "The Depot runs this place? But all these vendors. These small businesses—"

"Sharecroppers," spat Lilqua'tartian. "That and third-party sellers of Depot products."

"They used to be small businesses in the true sense," added Astra. "Then they went through what Lilqua'tartian's business went through. The Depot ran them out of business. Now, it's kind enough to negotiate deals with planets like this one to set up marketplaces for those same sellers to try to rebuild."

"But with Depot-set prices," said Dan as it sank in. "Pulsing blast."

"Maybe now you see why we stand against them," Astra replied. "Someone has to."

"And it isn't gonna be these slime trails," grouched Lilqua'tartian, gesturing with a spiny arm toward the sellers.

"They're trying to make a living," President Leviathan chided. "They're not the enemy. They're all potential allies."

"Potential my areoles!" The cactus grabbed the mug in front of Celeste and downed it, too.

"Why would anyone put up with this?" Vel asked. "Why would anyone tolerate the Depot buying up entire portions of planets and determining the prices for goods?"

Astra was the first to speculate. "Maybe they appreciate the convenience. Or it gives them a sense of security and protection. The Depot makes sure no scammers enter the markets to help preserve the credibility of the other sellers. The Depot has a whole task force dedicated to it."

Lilqua'tartian scoffed. "'Squadron' is the word you're looking for."

When the flippered woman returned, Alice ordered something called "peezal" without asking any questions. She felt fairly sure it would be pizza.

It was not.

But it was tacos, so all was well.

"Does the assembly know we're coming?" Vel asked.

"I've informed them," said Leviathan.

"And what do they think about the latest DeepService Team One dropping in?"

"Either someone will kill you or they won't."

Dan choked on his taico, which was pizza. "You don't know how they feel about us?"

Leviathan waved it off. "There's no 'they' in the true sense of the word. It's a bunch of individuals who feel various ways about everything. We've never had a unanimous vote. Even my election as president was hotly contested."

Alice wiped the sleeve of her jumpsuit across her mouth before speaking. "You gotta understand why we're a little jumpy. The Alliance has tried to kill us twice."

"Once," Astra said, "to be fair."

Alice rolled her eyes. "Definitely want to be *fair* about you shooting at us."

"My squad never did," Astra said.

Alice's attention jumped to Lilqua'tartian then back to Astra. "Bull. Shit. I *saw* this guy on Britannica. We spoke. He told me Susy's real name."

"That was you?" Vel's eyes shot hate at the cactus.

Lilqua'tartian held up his arms in surrender. "I'd only looked at her file. I didn't know she preferred Susy."

"I don't. I like Vel. Call me Vel. How hard is it?"

Alice leaned over the table toward Lilqua'tartian. "Susy gets like this. Don't take it personally."

"We were shooting at your client," Astra interjected. "Aubert Orleans. We were hoping to thwart the mission. Matching the Yoken from Star Cluster B with *anyone* outside of the containment barrier would be catastrophic."

"Ah, yeah, well, you don't have to worry about *that* anymore. The Depot cleaned it up."

Astra tilted her head to the side. "How so?"

"You don't know?" said Alice. "They eliminated the whole cluster. Poof. Blew it all up. Not a living soul."

"We were pawns in the game," Dan added. "It's clear now that they wanted to destroy their monstrous creation, but they needed a scapegoat, someone they could point to as a justification. And by saying how impossible it would be to match the Yoken, we unknowingly gave them what they needed."

"Nuh-uh," said Alice around a mouthful of peezal. "There's a difference between wanting to strangle someone and wanting to see their entire planet destroyed. I've wanted to strangle plenty of people back on Earth. That doesn't mean I want my whole planet destroyed and everyone I know kill—" She fell silent, remembering, then focused solely on her tacos.

Caid reached forward to place a holographic hand in the vicinity of her shoulder, but another holographic hand beat him to it. Caid and Celeste locked eyes and smiled.

Alice remained in a solemn state as President Leviathan waved goodbye to her flippered friend and the group left the restaurant. Vel could hardly begrudge Alice for that. The thought of the familiar disappearing, never to return, was too much to process in a matter of hours. The fact that Alice had managed to put it out of her mind for any time at all was an admirable show of resilience.

Or, you know, the product of a limited attention span.

With Alice checked out and their chain of command obsolete anyway, Vel took the lead. "Where is the assembly?" They were back in the crowded avenue, passing tables full of metal adornments and discounted footwear for the lucky few beings who evolved to have feet. "Wait, don't tell me. Guarly Dungeons. It's where the waitress suggested we go." Vel paused. "I suppose she was more than a waitress, then."

President Leviathan grinned.

As they rounded a corner, a fracas up ahead caused Vel's senses to go on high alert, but it was Dan who asked the obvious: "What's happening up there?"

The Alliance members appeared unfazed. "Looks like scammers," Astra replied.

"Maybe we should find an alternate route," Dan suggested as he watched a humanoid in hard armor beating a Jejoon to a pulp. The Jejoon begged for mercy, squeaking in pain after each hit.

"This is what you get, you little rotten scammer!" yelled the armored being. "Nobody discredits the Depot's marketplace!"

"I didn't— Eep! I followed the rules! I— Ouchy! Please, this is most uncalled— Oof!"

The Depot enforcer landed a blow to the Jejoon's marshmallow belly, knocking the wind right out of him.

Dan gave the altercation a wide berth as they passed, grimacing sympathetically with the injured Jejoon.

"Even for scammers, that seems harsh," Dan said.

"You believe a Jejoon would be a scammer?" barked Lilqua'tartian. "Shows how much you know."

"Then he's *not* a scammer?"

"Psh, course not. The Depot doesn't need to genuinely find scammers. They wait until someone reports one, then they pick a few merchants and bring down the hammer. Sends the same message as actually finding a problem."

"Christ," Alice whispered, blinking herself back to reality. "That ain't right. Jejoons are boring as a Latin mass, but they're peaceful." She made up her mind and turned to go back, figuring a physical altercation might be what the doctor ordered for her dark mood. But a hand gripped her wrist, stopping her. She turned to stare into the face of Vel.

Nope. Scar. President Leviathan.

"The only way to help him is to help them all."

"Nooo," Alice said. "I could also beat that enforcer's ass, throw the li'l dude on my shoulders, and get him somewhere safe. That would help him."

"That's not—"

"You have to be literal with her," Vel explained. "You'll get the hang of it." She shoved Alice forward, and the group moved on. They passed three more scammer crackdowns before they finally turned off onto a quieter side street.

Trash lined the edges of the walls, and they passed a huddle of sticklike beings with cellophane wings who passed a small spliff between them. With each inhale, their wings fluttered briefly, lifting them a few inches off the ground. One glared at the passing group and muttered something in a language Vel didn't recognize.

She did, however, recognize the tone of an insult, no matter the language. But just as it wasn't the time for Alice to play rescuer of the innocent, it also wasn't time for Vel to pick a fight.

Another sharp turn took them through an archway in the tall stone walls, and then they were going down, down, down a long set of stairs carved deep into the earth.

A strange texture appeared along the walls once the stairs stopped, and Alice crinkled her nose at it, reaching out a hand to touch on instinct. (Not survival instinct, though. It's generally best throughout the universe to not go around touching strange objects.)

Before her fingertips could reach it, a hand gripped her wrist.

"Those are bones," Leviathan said, and once it was clear the information had soaked in, she let go of Alice. "The dungeon is surrounded by catacombs."

"The Alliance picked a hell of a place to meet, then." Alice waited until Leviathan began on again then rubbed her wrist.

The noise began as a low drone but quickly grew louder. Fifty yards farther on, Alice began to make out individual voices.

None of them seemed happy.

A thick metal door appeared once they turned a final corner, but it was sitting wide open, and through it poured light and sound.

"If you try it, they'll know, and we'll all suffer for it!" shouted a hunchbacked being who stood on a long stone table that ran the length of the cavernous room. The being he shouted at had his paws on the floor but still had a good two feet on the other.

The shouts continued to assault them from the crowded chamber:

"You always say that, and you're always wrong!"

"If I have to hear you open your big, stupid jaw one more time …!"

"That's not what I said, you lump of space trash!"

Alice took it all in along with the décor of the space, which wasn't pretty.

After all, it was a dungeon.

Dan leaned in. "That's a hobsclamp table." She followed his gaze toward what appeared to be the world's most uncomfortable chain-mail hammock. "I didn't know those actually existed."

"Ah," Alice said, eyeing the dozens of spikes jutting from the floor below the chain mail, "me neither, obviously."

Similar apparatuses lined the walls of the large room, presumably moved out of the way for the assembly to gather without unnecessary injury or death.

The brightness of the room, however, limited the sinister tone of the torture devices and the barred cells set into the walls. It gave the space the feel of a haunted house at close—when the lights came up, the teenagers working there stored their fake chainsaws, shared cold cream to remove their makeup, and planned where they'd grab a late-night bite to eat.

"Weeks!" shouted a little thing with bug eyes and razor-sharp wings. "They haven't let up at all."

President Leviathan stepped forward. "What is this?"

Many eyes and eyelike organs turned her way, and those that didn't immediately did eventually after the bearer of said eyes and eyelike organs received an elbow, tentacle, or flapper from someone else.

Leviathan addressed Razor Wings again. "What hasn't let up in weeks?"

"The fraud sweeps. They've been worse than ever. A woman and her baby were killed during one last week, and more merchants than ever are having to start from scratch. Many have gone off-planet to look for other options, a marketplace that isn't built on Depot land."

"Good," said Leviathan, remaining planted inside the doorway. "I hope they find one. We could all use something like that."

"It wouldn't last for long," said the hunchbacked being. "Soon as the Depot got wind of it, they'd be there, cutting off supplies and travel, diverting it to a Depot planet. Like they always do."

Leviathan strode to the head of the stone stable. A wheel-shaped being rolled out of the high-backed chair, in front of which President Leviathan planted her feet and didn't sit down. "Do we know what's sparked these fraud sweeps?"

"Do we ever?" spat the hunchback.

Leviathan remained calm. "Yes, sometimes we do, Mickurty."

"We can guess, sure. But who's to say we're right?"

This was not how Alice had imagined the assembly would speak to the acting president, but she liked Mickurty's spirit. It reminded her of Dan.

"The fraud sweeps will slow," Leviathan replied. "They always do. In the meantime, what do we have in place to support active Alliance members who are caught up in it?"

"Support?" Mickurty spat aggressively for no reason other than he seemed to be one hell of a mood.

"Yes. We are an *alliance*, are we not?" Leviathan arched her brows. "What does that mean to you if not supporting each other in the face of a greater enemy?"

"I'd expect there'd be some loyalty, too," replied the hunchback, "but instead we have a traitor in our midst!"

The room exploded with noise at the accusation, and Alice folded her arms across her chest, watching. When someone appeared next to her, she turned, expecting it to be Dan again.

"Wuulg!" She jumped, reaching for her blaster when she saw the giant cockroach next to her.

No, not *quite* a cockroach.

It stood on its hind legs, which might've been its only

legs for all she knew of its alien anatomy, and while it had the same color and body shape as the massive American cockroaches she used to swat out of the air with a rolled-up newspaper, its face was strangely human. "Don't worry," it said in a deep voice that caused her mind to assume it was a male, "it's always this chaotic."

Alice let her hand fall from her blaster. "Oh yeah?"

"Especially when there are sweeps. The Alliance has billions of members, but one single fraud bust, and everyone assumes their business will be next."

"Billions of members? That big?"

The roach shrugged, which Alice found slightly nightmarish. "It's a big universe. Gus." He offered a spindly leg, and her Southern manners overrode the ick factor. They shook.

"Alice. If there are billions of members, how do they decide who gets to attend the assembly?"

"Gets to?" Gus laughed. "More like has to. No one wants to be Alliance leadership. Her least of all." He pointed to President Leviathan, who was rolling her eyes at that very moment. "She's our first president. We did a committee thing for a while, but it always ended in gridlock."

"They're, like, elected, then?"

"Whenever the assembly can get itself together enough to hold an election, yes."

"How often is that?"

"Hard to say."

"Right. Time stuff."

Gus eyed her closely. "You're new to all this, aren't you?"

"Relatively."

He laughed, his underbelly vibrating. "Fair enough."

As the arguing continued in front of them, Dan appeared on Alice's other side, "So here's where I'm stuck —" He noticed the cockroach. "Oh, hello."

Alice thumbed at her new acquaintance. "Dan, this is Gus. Gus, Dan."

"Pleasure," Dan said. "Sorry to interrupt." And then he pulled Alice a few steps away for a private conversation. "Here's where I'm stuck: are we joining up with the Alliance?"

Alice watched the chaos, half of her wanting very much to consider herself a part of it. "I don't think we've decided that yet."

"But the Depot are definitely the bad guys."

Alice turned her head quickly to get a read on him. "Sure as shit. I thought that was pretty clear as soon as they blew up a whole star cluster."

"Yes, of course. But—" He grimaced in the direction of the table, where a tubular constrictor was wrapping itself around Mickurty, squeezing the life out of him while Razor Wings attempted to fight it off. "Are they not *also* bad guys?"

"I can't believe you're still hung up on good-guy-bad-guy stuff. But fine. There can't be that many bad guys. There have to be good guys."

"Statistically, yes, I believe you. The universe tends to keep a balance naturally. But maybe the good guys are somewhere else?"

Alice clapped a hand on his shoulder. "You're overthinking it. The Alliance is a little chaotic, sure, but they're not the Depot, and they're all we got right now."

Caid inserted himself into the private conversation. "Would you look at the diversity of thought here? Wow! What a furnace for innovation!"

"See?" Alice said to Dan. "Caid isn't worried. Maybe you should give yourself a break. Take a deep breath."

"Anytime is a good time for deep breathing," Caid added.

"No, it's not," Dan said. "Have you ever tried *deep breathing* while something with big teeth chased you? Not great. Shallow breathing is better."

"But there's nothing with big teeth here," Alice said.

"There." Dan pointed to a being that was *mostly* large, sharp teeth, whom Alice hadn't yet noticed.

"Ah, well, it seems friendly enough."

Razor Wings had successfully convinced the tubular constrictor to let Mickurty go, and the hunchback crawled off the table, coughing and clutching his middle.

President Leviathan cleared her throat, but it did nothing to slow the swell of discontent this time. "The more united we are," she said, raising her voice, "the more power we have. We must remember that—"

"I'll be zapped if I do *anything* to make the Depot sweep my business!" A being with seriously sea urchin qualities slammed one of its larger spines down on the table as it shouted at the president. A small valve at the top of it puckered as it spoke, and Alice very wrongly assumed that was its mouth.

"You're forgetting," Leviathan replied, "that many of those caught up in the sweeps have done *nothing* to warrant the brutality."

"I'd bet they did something," the spiny urchin replied. "Remember when Wonk Tromper got caught in the sweeps and everyone was so indignant about it? Not a day later it came out that he *had* been scamming. All those high-ticket items that lured people to his booth were holograms! He even tried to sell a few as physical items before he was caught. I have half a mind to *thank* the Depot for staying on top of the problem! Scammers make the rest of us look—"

But what it made everyone else look was never disclosed, because the being that was mostly teeth waddled up behind the speaker, opened its massive maw, and chomped the spiny thing down in two bites.

"Breathe deeply, my ass," Dan muttered, his heart racing as his spine curled, his body ready to roll him into a ball at a moment's notice.

President Leviathan exhaled and rubbed at her forehead, reminding Alice strangely of her own mother each time a call came in that one of the Luck boys needed to be picked up from the sheriff's office.

But Janice Luck was dead now.

Leviathan turned to look at the rest of her crew and the Depot turncoats, all still huddled by the dungeon door, threw her hands up, and called, "Welcome to the Assembly of Independent Businesses."

CHAPTER
FOURTEEN

Evolution loves competition. Survival of the fittest and all. But sometimes the fittest being isn't the one that is able to successfully reproduce most frequently. Sometimes the fittest being is the one with the big, sharp teeth and not a single fuck left to give.

President Leviathan recognized that possibility when Hunny Hodgl Rit chomped D'Iz Powt in two bites at the Alliance assembly table.

Hunny Hodgl Rit, often referred to simply as "The Teeth," had been a valued Alliance member for longer than Lev could recall, and the president was fairly sure that the toothy thing was the most ancient being in the room, holograms excluded. Or maybe even holograms included. It was hard to say because Hunny Hodgl Rit never spoke, so she couldn't relate her story. Many speculated that it was because she predated speech in the universe. Many others speculated that she was merely of low intelligence.

Those in the latter group were generally eaten by

Hunny Hodgl Rit, selecting out *that* theory and leaving only the fittest: that she was ancient as hell.

Either way, Lev wasn't upset that Hunny Hodgl Rit had eaten D'Iz Powt. Powt was mostly anus, and always acted like it. He would've fomented rebellion within the rebellion soon enough.

The uproar of the room returned as Hunny Hodgl Rit retreated, still chewing her snack, and Lev realized she was losing the room. She'd hoped to have a little more peace before announcing the first major item on her agenda, but hope and expectation were two separate things. Lev hadn't *expected* the Assembly to be any less chaotic—it never was. But a girl *could* hope.

"If you haven't already noticed, I've brought guests with me today."

If the volume of the room lowered, it was only by a hair.

Not for the first time, Lev wished she had a gavel.

"May I have your attention, please?"

No change in volume.

Lilqua'tartian appeared at her side. "Allow me." He aimed his blaster at the ceiling and pulled the trigger. A portion of rock over their heads exploded, showering dust and sharp debris down on those in attendance. "Make me do it again and this whole place could collapse. If ya think I give a single spine off my ass about dying, yer messing with the wrong Pokonolio! Now shut up and listen to yer president!"

Alice brushed away a crumble of dust from her cheek. "I think I'm warming to this prickly psycho."

President Leviathan didn't entirely or even partially approve of Lilqua'tartian's methods, but she couldn't argue that they were effective. The room was now silent.

"Thank you." She paused to regroup, then let a calm smile blossom on her face. Or that was what she thought she was doing. No one else noticed a smile. She simply looked slightly less lethal than usual.

"I've brought guests with me today. They're crucial to our mission, and I expect you to trust and respect them as I do."

Hunny Hodgl Rit belched from the back of the room, making the idea of respect seem like a good one.

"Our guests were recently the official DeepService Team One, but they have defected."

"All due respect," said a furry creature in the chair next to where D'Iz Powt had sat before he was eaten. "And I mean *all due respect*." The furry thing shot a look over its shoulder at The Teeth. Hunny Hodgl Rit hadn't moved, so it went on. "You say they've defected from the Depot, but that doesn't mean they've aligned with the Alliance. There are plenty of neutral parties in the universe."

"Fair point, Trubidee," Leviathan replied, and the furry thing exhaled the breath it'd been holding. "I believe everyone has a right to peacefully exist outside of both the Depot and the Alliance if they choose, but I brought this group here in hopes that they would better understand our mission and decide to help us. I can't say this assembly has made a convincing argument for itself thus far."

Hunny Hodgl Rit made to approach the table again, but President Leviathan shook her head subtly to indicate that The Teeth's services weren't needed.

"It's my pleasure to introduce them to you. Here we have Caid Sonorian, an organic hologram similar to our much beloved Celeste. He's worked with DeepService Team One since before it was called that. His loyalty has always been to those on his crew, the people, not the Depot, which is why I trust him. He cares deeply, and one who cares deeply cannot stay loyal to authoritarian entities."

Caid clasped his hands to his heart and bowed in humble appreciation for her generous introduction.

"And here we have Dan Zone, originally from the planet Pangoliarch. He's served the Depot indirectly through his position at the Ministry of Weapons and Culture, one of the so-called neutral departments that reports back to the Depot. However, his loyalty doesn't extend past betrayal, and the Depot has betrayed him. He's a valuable resource, and I hope he will choose to serve the Alliance's cause of security through diversity."

Dan's arms were folded over his chest during the entire introduction, and they didn't move once all eyes were on him.

"And here we have Susy Machiavelli. She and I seem to be the same person from parallel universes. She, too, was a warrior where she came from, and she's one of the most determined and savvy minds I've encountered in this universe. We abducted her from her crew prior to this, and it was through those moments together that she was able to see the truth and convince her crew to open their eyes as well."

Alice snuck a look at Vel, who appeared murderous.

Ah, well, no one likes to be manipulated. Though Alice had been the victim of manipulations more often than any surviving person should and knew it was no personal failing to be manipulated, perhaps this was a novel experience for Vel.

"We thank you for your clearheadedness," President Leviathan said, not realizing she was lucky to be alive after implying what she had. "And lastly, I would like to introduce everyone to Alice Luck, the captain of the team and a native Texan."

Gasps from the crowd caused Alice to perk up, ready to fight, though it quickly became apparent that she'd read the room wrong.

"Can it be?" squeaked Razor Wings. "How in the multiverse did you find yourself a Texan?"

"The Depot found her. They recruited from their headquarters there."

"It cannot be!" came a shout from the crowd. "Texas was destroyed by the bombs!"

"The whats?" Alice said, looking around for the person who'd spoken.

President Leviathan saw what was happening, and while she hadn't known about any bombs herself, she did know the precarious state her home planet of Blerg VFP69 had existed in for a long time. She also knew that bombs were to planets as cancer was to organic beings—inevitable if nothing else got 'em first.

Now wasn't the time to send Alice into a spiral. "She has all the characteristics we need, plus, she seems to have the Gift."

The room fell silent.

Alice looked around, having failed to find the being who mentioned the bombs. Now it looked like no one would follow up with her. Instead, they were staring. Staring so, so hard.

She blinked. "What'd you say? You have a gift for me?"

"She was born to lead us," Lev continued. "That much is clear."

"The fuck?" Alice muttered. She turned to Vel, who seemed similarly confused by the idea.

Razor Wings piped up, "Do you concede your role as Alliance president and propose a new election?"

Alice took a step back toward the door.

Then another.

And another.

Dan grabbed her arm. "Where are you going?" he whispered.

"What?"

"You're backing toward the door."

She appeared genuinely surprised. "Am I?"

From the head of the table, Lev replied, "I'm not conceding my position yet, but if the consensus at this assembly is that I ought to so that Alice Luck can take the role, then it's my duty to do so."

Alice shook free from Dan's grasp. "Nope. Nuh-uh." Her soles scratched across grit on the stone floors, and she boot-scooted farther away from the decision making.

"Hey!" shouted Lilqua'tartian, jabbing an arm toward her. "Where do you think you're going?"

Alice froze. "Bathroom?"

Lev narrowed her eyes at Alice, then addressed the assembly. "Talk amongst yourselves and try not to kill each other. I need a private moment with my guests."

"You're not in trouble," Caid crooned softly to Alice. "I sense your sympathetic nervous system on high alert. Breathe deeply to remind it that you're not in trouble."

"I think she *is* in trouble, though," Dan said. "We all are if we fall in with these people."

"We were in trouble the moment we signed with the Depot," Vel griped. "We just didn't know it at the time."

"Come with me," Lev said, addressing the smaller group. "There are a few things you all must know."

CHAPTER
FIFTEEN

By the time the group reached the private room in the dungeons, Alice had well and truly worked herself into a lather. Before President Leviathan could get a word out, Alice let 'er rip.

"You got me all wrong, bucko. I ain't here to lead *anything*. I joined DeepService Team One to *escape* responsibility, not take on more of it. The hell is all this talk about me being *president*? I haven't agreed to jack shit! I don't even understand how any of this works! If you think I have *any* desire to lead the Suicide Squad from space out there, you're outta your mind! The teethy one seems okay, and the little gopher thing was adorable, but the rest? No way. I don't trust 'em farther than I could kick them!"

President Leviathan waited patiently for the Texan to finish, then said, "Are you done?"

"Done with this shit, yeah."

Lilqua'tartian stood by the door to the small, empty room. It may have housed torture equipment at one point, but all that remained were a few shackles dangling on rusty chains on the far wall. The space even lacked chairs or a table, so Alice, her former crew, and President Leviathan stood facing each other in the center of it. Caid positioned himself to Alice and Lev's side, as a referee might between the captains at a coin toss, though he could only verbally intervene if things truly went south.

That didn't seem likely to anyone, though, because Leviathan was unfazed by Alice's mood.

"What do you know about Star Cluster A?" the president asked.

The question was intriguing enough to hijack Alice's attention from her plans to shoot off Lilqua'tartian's arm again and make a break for it. "It was, um, only the beginning?"

At that, President Leviathan smiled, and it even came across as such. "So you discovered the message."

"Yeah. When I dropped—" *A vial of alien jizz.* "Yes, I found it while looking for clues. That's a thing I do. Did you write it?"

"No. But I know the man who did. I was the one who warned him about it."

Vel stepped forward. "And *what* did you warn him about? What happened with Star Cluster A?"

"As I already told you, I was part of the early test missions for the Depot back in the 1980s, Earth time," Leviathan said. "They'd experienced recent success colonizing what is now Britannica with the help of a man called Strumpkins, and they wanted to take their experiments to new places. I—"

"Hold on," Dan said, squinting at her. "How did you used to work for them and then become their client?"

"New identity. I've had my prints and biometrics

altered since then for security reasons. Most Alliance members have."

"But you look the same as you used to."

"So does she." Lev nodded toward Vel. "A lot of people look the same. Evolution is not as creative as you'd think, and there are plenty of connected universes parallel to this one."

"Sounds like the Depot has a type," Alice added. "First they hired you, then your duplicate in Susy, then they hired you again as a client, thinking you were a different you."

That seemed to trip up Leviathan for a moment. "Perhaps. You raise an interesting point. I'll have to think more about that."

"Could also be a random coincidence," said Caid, who had, only seconds before, turned into Charlie Chaplin.

All eyes lingered on him for a moment. He raised a good point. Plenty of random to go around lately.

Dan ran a quick internal check for jitters, found none, then addressed Leviathan. "You were telling us about Star Cluster A."

"I was on the mission to Star Cluster A," she said. "It was the first test mission. At the time, it wasn't known as Star Cluster A. It was simply a portion of the universe, not unlike any other. My crew and I visited two planets to gather biological specimens. There was a particular phenomenon that the Depot was interesting in investigating in both populations."

"What kind of phenomenon?" asked Dan.

"Large penises."

"Ha!" said Alice. "A space mission to see why folks had big dicks?"

"Yes," said Leviathan plainly. "What else do you think drives exploration on Earth?"

Alice opened her mouth to respond but had nothing to say.

"As part of our mission, we gathered biological samples and returned them to the Depot headquarters. We had no idea of their intended use.

"Only when we were sent back to both planets with frozen specimens did I start to question what was going on. And then the first generation of Havirshanks were born, and it became clear to me what the mission was all along. And I'd played a part in it.

"Females on each planet were injected with the fertilized eggs. A few months later, the babies ate their way free of their mothers. Devoured them from the inside out. That was when I knew we'd done something horrible."

Alice cringed. "If that didn't tell ya, nothing would."

"As you might imagine, the Havirshanks quickly became a problem on both planets. They didn't grow less murderous after leaving the womb. Within a few generations, they'd made both planets inhospitable. I was there when word reached the Depot. My liaison, Richard, hadn't shut the door at headquarters, and I heard it all. The Depot leadership he spoke with predicted that the Havirshanks wouldn't be able to leave their planets, would be stranded there and eventually die out from lack of natural resources and/or cannibalism. No one expected what *actually* happened."

"Which was?" asked Dan.

"The Havirshanks made it off-planet. By the time my crew returned, they were many generations into space travel, and every planet within two light-years of theirs had been colonized and tainted, if not ecologically destroyed. The only positive was that they hadn't learned how to travel via space fold, so the damage was fairly localized. You can probably guess what the Depot did next."

"Containment barrier around the cluster?" Caid suggested, looking like himself again.

"Indeed," said Leviathan. "And to play it safe, they threw everything within ten light-years of the planets in there. Innocents put in a cage with monsters. Not for long, though. Just long enough for the Depot to decide what to do with them."

"I have a feeling I know what they decided," Dan said gravely.

"You probably do. But first, the Depot made absolutely sure these monsters couldn't be used for any greater purpose."

"How do you know that?" Vel said. "No way the Depot let you into that discussion."

"Richard told me. He *was* in on the discussions, and he was horrified by them. He confided in me because he had no one else. The liaisons are kept isolated outside of their duties. Sometimes they get a single android companion, but those are hardly more than spies for the Depot themselves.

"In the end, the Havirshanks were deemed too uncontrollable to be of any strategic use, and that was when the Depot made the call. Richard came to me to let me know, to tell me to get as far away from Blerg VFP69 and what was then known as Star Cluster A as I could, and to never return. The Depot was not who he'd thought they were. Not who any of us thought they were. I did what he told me, I left my home behind forever, and

I never heard from him again. Presumably they killed him."

"Seems a safe bet," said Vel, unsympathetically.

"Nobody outside of those involved with the Depot mission knew about the fate of Star Cluster A. They kept it secret, and by creating such a large containment barrier, they guaranteed that no one outside of it had brushed up against the horror of the Havirshanks. A twenty-light-year void in the universe is somewhat common and unremarkable.

"What I still don't understand," Leviathan continued, "is why they kept Star Cluster B around for so long, allowed it to get a reputation before they destroyed it."

"From the folks we met in it," said Alice, "they were bad, but not Havirshank-bad. A little rapey—okay, a *lot* rapey—and the worst sort of parents, but the children didn't devour their mothers. They were Havirshank Light."

Leviathan took it in quietly, her eyes narrowed in deep thought. "So perhaps the Depot believed the people of Star Cluster B *could* be controlled."

"It sure seemed like it," Vel replied. "I suspect they sent us on that mission for reconnaissance, not a true matching expedition."

"Likely. But the Depot miscalculated if it thought the universe would back the annihilation of an entire star cluster. Word has spread, and half the people I've spoken with can't believe the Depot would do something like this. It's opened up eyes that were shut for a very long time."

"And the other half?" Dan said. "Where do they fall?"

Leviathan frowned. "You've spent your life learning about various cultures. Surely you've learned a thing or two about how populations shake out when confronted with cruel and powerful entities. Not to mention, the Depot has launched an all-out propaganda campaign since the elimination, and unfortunately, it's proving to be effective."

"What could they possibly say?" Alice demanded. "They blew up half a galaxy!" She didn't technically know that to be true because she still confused solar system, galaxy, and universe, and had no idea where a star cluster fit on the scale. But no one corrected her exaggeration.

"The Depot claims the containment barrier was breached. As the narrative goes, inhabitants of Star Cluster B were escaping in trickles and planning an all-out onslaught on the barrier so they could finally be free to loot and rape around the galaxy. The Depot engaged them in peacekeeping efforts while fixing the breaches. The Depot claims it was ultimately the efforts of Star Cluster B, led by the Yoken, to blast a hole through the barrier with a series of fusion bombs that backfired and led to the annihilation. Before the Depot could do a thing about it, the fusion bombs created a cascade inside the containment barrier that eliminate all life within it."

"I have to hand it to them," said Vel. "It's brilliant reframing. A perfectly sympathetic story."

"Exactly. And it's why we're losing the information war against them. According to their tales, they keep saving everyone again and again. People like being saved. It keeps them from worrying about saving themselves. We're fighting a war over the narrative more than anything physical."

"Hate to be that guy," said Dan, "but it doesn't sound like the Alliance is winning on *any* front."

"We're in a slump," Leviathan admitted. "We could use a few improbable things to happen for us to get the upper hand, but—" She shot Caid a glance. "He can probably tell you that improbable things are happening all the time lately."

"More than usual," said Caid, "that's for sure. Proof that hope can never die."

"Always a chance for repair," added Celeste.

Their eyes met. "So long as one still exists," Caid murmured serenely, "there's a chance for repair."

Alice looked back and forth between them. "The hell is this shit?"

"It's not just the holograms," Dan added. "I've sensed the improbability myself. I suffer from quantum jitters."

Leviathan's eyebrows rose. "Really? And have they been bad lately?"

"On and off, but not in the usual moments. Events that might be considered improbable aren't triggering them, but events that seem ordinary and expected are."

"A shift in probability waves?"

"That would explain it, but I'd hate for it to be the case."

"Hmm." Leviathan inspected Dan closely. "Usually I would, too, but considering the Alliance's predicament, we could use a little luck."

"Huh?" said Alice, looking around for who'd said her name. She'd lost herself in watching the holograms make eyes at each other and had tumbled down a not-totally-unpleasant rabbit hole of imagining holographic sex.

The rest of the small room was staring at her now, and she felt she ought to say something clever. Instead, she went with: "You said my name?"

"I did," Leviathan replied. "Perhaps this is a sign. An improbable one, sure, but that's even better. We needed luck, and we got it in you. A native Texan who ends up at our assembly right when things are looking dire. You've led your crew out of tough spots and escaped the Depot's detection. You convinced a Depot operating system to rebel and let us go free. I've never heard of anyone like that."

"She also triggered my jitters pretty much constantly before the probabilities shifted," Dan said. "I suspect I was allergic to her."

"Taking that as a compliment," Alice said. "But hold up, Pres, 'cause you got me all wrong. I don't know what I'm doing."

"And yet you succeed. Don't you find that interesting?"

"Not really," said Alice. "That's how the world works. Sometimes you get lucky."

"Or perhaps," Dan added, his almond eyes growing with excitement, which set Alice on edge in a fun kind of way, "it's how *your* world works. It doesn't happen that way for other people. I've heard of this phenomenon before. The Improbable Birth."

"No, no, no," Alice said, waving off the idea. "My mom *definitely* wasn't a virgin. She had six kids before having me."

"That's not what I mean," Dan said. "Wait, what do you think I meant?"

"Immaculate— Never mind. What did you mean?"

Dan pushed through his confusion. "Improbable Birth. I wasn't sure it was real, but maybe it is. As the legend goes, if a person is born who by all odds shouldn't be, their existence can make the probability waves around them waver more at a quantum level. So strange things happen. Unexpected things. Lucky things." He and Leviathan locked eyes, and the understanding passed between them. "You might be an Improbable Birth, Alice."

She held up her hands to slow his roll. "Easy, friend. Let's not get ahead of ourselves. First off, *plenty* of people are born on Leap Day."

"Is that when you were born?" Dan said, quickening his roll.

"Yeah, but like I said, there are a *lot* of people born then. And I'm sure a good amount were also born at 11:11 a.m. on Leap Day, just like me."

Dan's hairless brows rose.

"And the fact that I was born breech with no major complications for me or my mother is nothing to get worked up about. Medicine has come a long way, ya know?"

Vel opened her mouth, but Dan silenced her with a hand on her arm. Best to let Alice keep speaking in moments like this.

"And where I'm from, car births like mine aren't *that* uncommon. The hospital is an hour away, and the midwife broke three of her toes that morning when an airplane part felt out of the sky onto her foot, so *obviously* my mother had to go to the hospital rather than have a home birth. But, ya know, car babies happen! Look it up! The fact that Kiefer Sutherland happened to be riding past that stretch of highway on a cross-country motorcycle tour, saw my mother's car on the side of the road, and helped deliver me is a *little* out of the ordinary, sure, but anyone would've stopped to offer assistance."

Leviathan exhaled in a whoosh. "You consider that a *probable* birth?"

"Reckon so," said Alice. "Same sorta thing happened with all my brothers, too. Not Kiefer Sutherland, but some of the other stuff. Buck was delivered by Meryl

Streep in line for a Ferris wheel. Texas State Fair, 1984. Look it up. Famous actors deliver babies *not infrequently*."

By the time Alice ran out of steam, Vel had her arms crossed over her chest, and President Leviathan was covering her mouth in disbelief.

"Is she stupid?" barked Lilqua'tartian from the doorway. "Seriously, what's her deal?"

It was Leviathan who answered. "She's built for improbabilities. Better than any of us, I think. She truly is the one to lead us during this time."

"Ugh," Alice said. "That wasn't my point."

"It's true," Dan said, viewing at his former captain with new eyes. "Think about it, Alice: when improbable things become probable, Caid becomes unstable in his form. I get jitters at inappropriate times. Vel runs into her parallel self and develops an inferiority complex—"

"I do not."

"But you," Dan continued, "you're *thriving*."

Alice scoffed. "I'd hardly call this thriving."

"What *would* you call thriving, then?"

Alice thought about it. "Spending the rest of my life on Jaspariampt with all the money the Depot owes me."

"Please, you would hate that," Dan replied. "Three months in and you'd be ready to jump off-planet."

"You don't know— Okay, fine. What's your point?"

"Thought he made that pretty clear," said Lilqua'tartian.

Alice shot him a nobody-asked-you look.

"Alice," Dan said, remembering her preference for information a five-year-old would understand, "what if you ended up in this exact moment to lead the Alliance to victory?"

She tilted her head back on a deep inhale, pouting her

lips as her mind raced through the possibilities of her next move. Finally, she hit on one she liked. "Yeah, okay. You got me. Maybe I am the woman for this moment, because I know what we need to do. But first, I need a ship." She addressed President Leviathan. "Can you get me that?"

"I certainly can."

"Just for us," Alice added, thumbing at Caid, Vel, and Dan. "We're going to need stealth for this. The fewer people the better, but I need my crew with me."

"Absolutely. I'll get that arranged right away, and then I'll inform the assembly that you've agreed to step into a leadership role."

"Yeah, totally," Alice said.

She could feel Vel's skeptical gaze on her, but thankfully, her former lieutenant didn't voice whatever suspicion she was harboring.

It was only natural for Vel to believe something strange was afoot. Because even in the most improbable environment, Alice Luck would *never* think more than one step ahead.

Which meant that the next step Alice intended to take was an obvious one.

CHAPTER
SIXTEEN

President Leviathan delivered on the ship, and soon Alice, Dan, Caid, and Vel had boarded the small craft. Astra Blum had assured them that it was a perfectly reliable ship and that they would find the operating system entirely obedient.

Alice already hated it.

Once on the bridge—and most of this ship was bridge, with only two additional bunk rooms and one shared bathroom—the group fell into their old roles easily. Alice took the captain's seat because, after all, she was about to be the president of the Alliance. It wasn't nearly as comfortable as the one on *Emergence*, and she added it to her growing list of grievances.

Vel assumed the seat on Alice's left, and Dan settled in by the weapon controls. Caid chose to meditate, and hovered at the back of the bridge, slowly rising and falling with each deep breath.

"Systems ready?" Vel asked.

A flat, masculine voice responded. "Affirmative. *Pythagoras* ready for liftoff at your word."

A strange, garbled sound drew Alice's attention to Dan, who shook himself like a dog after a bath.

"Jitters?" she asked.

"Minor, but yes."

She looked around. "From what?"

"No idea."

Vel took a guess. "You said you're getting jitters at probable things lately, right? Maybe *Pythagoras* being predictably reliable set you off."

Pythagoras, Alice thought bitterly. *What a stupid ship name.* "What's your name?" she asked the operating system.

"Wiser."

Alice crinkled her nose, but Vel added, "This is a Wiser 5600. Not a Depot system, which is an obvious plus, but about the most efficient we could hope for."

"He sounds like a fucking square."

"He is," said Vel, making it clear she felt a different way about that.

"Whatever," Alice said, feeling itchy. "Let's get out of here."

"We're ready at your word," said Vel. "Presumably you have a *plan* for where we're going. Not a full one, of course, but you know the next step. Let Wiser know, and we'll begin." She didn't blink as her gaze bored a hole through Alice.

The look was a challenge, Alice knew. Vel was daring her to do the stupid thing that they all, on some level, knew she was going to do.

That didn't stop her from doing it. "Wiser?"

"Yes, Captain?"

She gagged a little at his suck-up voice. "Just call me

Da— Actually, no. You'd make it lame." She shook her head mournfully. "Goddammit, I miss Allura."

"A destination?" Dan prompted.

"Right, right. Wiseass, take us to the farthest reaches of the universe, please!"

"Huh?" said Dan, before another pulse of jitters ran through him.

"I knew it," muttered Vel.

"Yes, Captain," said Wiser.

Liftoff.

Once they were through the rough patch of the planet's atmosphere, Dan spun his chair toward Alice, appearing slightly the worse for wear with puffy eyes and hunched shoulders after two short bouts of the jitters. "What are we doing, exactly?"

"What does it sound like?" Vel replied. "Alice is doing what she always does."

"You say that like it's a bad thing, Susy. I always do this because it always works!"

Vel scoffed. "Running away always works? *That's* why you keep ending up in situations where you have to run away? Because it's such an effective technique?"

"It's never let me down yet," Alice snapped.

"We're heading to the farthest reaches of the universe to avoid your problems! How does that look like success to you?!"

"Sure, it's not *prestigious* like you would prefer, Susy, but not everything has to earn you medals!"

Caid appeared between their chairs, cutting the tension. "Habit patterns are a funny thing," he said dreamily.

"Not now," Vel and Alice both said.

A shadow of hurt passed across his face, but he backed off, giving them the space they desired.

"Were we at the same assembly back there?" Alice asked, looking from Vel to Dan. "Those people are a *mess*."

"They're the only ones with a chance of defeating the Depot's stranglehold on this universe," Vel said.

"Agree to disagree, then, because a plate of crispy tacos has a better chance of going uneaten in a boys' dorm than they have of beating the Depot." She got to her feet. "Y'all. What does *any* of this have to do with me? With us? Why should I have to fight the Depot? I never asked to be a part of this. I thought I was gonna be hawking printer supplies and posterboard when I applied. Shitty, sure, but easy. I could collect my minimum-wage paycheck, get my fiancé off my back about finding a job, and then blow my minimum-wage paycheck as soon as I got off the clock. But instead, I'm hopping around space, being recruited to the universe's biggest dick-slinging competition between the Depot and the Alliance, and—oh yeah—everything I ever knew and loved on my home planet has disappeared in the meantime! Hasn't the universe asked enough of me already? Hasn't it taken enough? And what has it given me? Nothing but a whole heap of problems and dangers and responsibilities I didn't ask for! Maybe we should've let ourselves get banished after the failed trial mission. At least we'd be free of all this drama. At least I wouldn't have an assembly of nutjobs trying to make me president of the shitshow because of where I was born." Her cheeks burned, and the sensation of blood rushing to her head was some small comfort. "Fuck yeah, we're getting as far away from this as possible. It's not my problem. It's not *our* problem! Y'all are the only people I have left, so I'm taking you with me. I suggest you get over it. Maybe even thank me for getting us this whack-ass ship!"

"My humble appreciation, Captain."

"Shut the fuck up, Wiser!"

The bridge fell silent, and Alice felt the first tingling of her panic and fear turning to shame. As she looked around for where a gal could get a drink around there, Vel spoke.

"For fear of sounding like Caid, have you ever considered that maybe your problems will follow you wherever you go?"

Caid perked up. "That's so insightful, Vel."

She glared at him. "I'm not talking metaphorically. I'm talking literally. The universe may be expanding, sure, but so is the Depot, and at a faster rate. We might be able to find somewhere to hide that the Depot hasn't messed with yet, but eventually, they'll be there. And when they are, they'll recognize their favorite fugitives. What then?"

"You know we'll die eventually, right, Susy?" Alice spared Caid a glance. "Oh right. Sorry. My point is that I know *I'm* gonna die sometime, and I'm going to do whatever I can to make sure it's in old age with a cold drink in one hand, a hunk of cheese in the other, and something soft beneath my ass. That's it. That's what success looks like *for me*. I only have to avoid the Depot long enough to grow old and die. There's gotta be somewhere in this universe that fits the bill."

"What if there isn't?" said Vel.

Alice huffed. "I'm getting a lot of negativity from you, Susy. I thought you were resourceful. If you want to succeed here, I'm gonna need more can-do than can't-do from you."

Vel's jaw clenched tight.

"Wiseass."

Silence.

Alice grunted. "Fine. Wiser!"

"Yes, Captain?"

"You got one of those slots where you can send me shit I want?"

"Yes, Captain. Is there a particular type of feces you wish me to send you?"

Alice dragged a hand over her face. "This guy. No. I don't want literal poop. I want a beer."

"Alcoholic beverages are not within the programming of this ship."

Alice steadied herself on the back of her captain's chair, feeling her knees go weak.

"Oh no," said Dan. "Her eyes. Look at her eyes. She's looking for an escape hatch." He jumped in front of her, ready to tackle if necessary. "There's nowhere to go. If you try to get off the ship while we're in the vacuum of space, we'll all die. Please, Captain. Have a seat. You don't look well."

Alice collapsed into her chair, shaking slightly.

"Wiser," said Dan, "get her a block of cheese, stat!"

Alice stared up at the bottom of the top bunk, crossing her eyes to make the texture of the wood above her swirl and blur. She uncrossed them. Then she crossed them harder.

It was day two aboard *Pythagoras,* and Alice had run out of ways to distract herself. Wiser had done his best, presenting her with various games on a tablet, but some were too simple, and others she didn't understand or were text-based. She spent eight hours playing a game called Black Hole, which was essentially the snake game she'd played on her TI-89 calculator in high school, before she hit a wall where she thought she might throw up if she played a minute more of it.

The problem was that as soon as she stopped playing, she would remember.

Earth. Home. The cat that visited her on Jacob's doorstep each morning with a little bell around his neck and one missing eye. George Galway, the old cowboy who greeted her at every livestock show, fed her the local gossip, and let her pet the barrel-racing horses when no one was looking. The familiar sights and sounds of her local café and bakery where she'd kill the hours during her blessed period of unemployment, when Jacob thought she was pounding the pavement.

It was all gone. In the blink of an eye, in the jump of a single large time fold—poof—she'd missed out on all of it forever.

Tensions were at a boiling point among the group. Vel was moodier than ever, which made her horrifyingly quiet most of the time, like a loaded gun with a silencer. Every time Alice had encountered Dan in the last two days, his eyes were bulging from his head, and he would blurt things like "IT'S GONNA BE FINE," when nobody had said otherwise.

Caid was, perhaps, the worst of all. When he wasn't changing rapidly into more and more obscure Old Hollywood actors, he was trying to wring feelings from everyone. "Let's talk about it" and "this much uninterrupted time with our thoughts is a gift" had been uttered more than once, and the most recent occurrence of it was why Alice and Vel were locked away in their small bunk room. Poor Dan had nowhere to escape to.

"Christ," Alice said, feeling dizzy from crossing and uncrossing her eyes. The ship was fully stocked with fresh clothing, and Alice had gone for a casual green cotton jumpsuit to match her eyes. It felt a little like wearing a onesie, which was why she loved it. "How long does it take to get to the farthest reaches of space?"

From the top bunk, Vel grunted. "I've never met anyone with less of an understanding of how the universe works."

"You must not've met any flat-Earthers."

Despite her moodiness, Vel said, "Any what?"

"Flat-Earthers. Did y'all not have those on your version of Blerg VFP69? Ah, well, they're folks who think Earth is flat, and you can walk off the end of it if you try. And the universe we see in the sky is, like, a dome. A painted dome."

"Ah," said Vel knowingly. "We had similarly idiotic people. They believed the Earth was a balloon that could be popped. They protested against all drilling, for fear that someone would pop it. They marched against shovels."

"You think they're still alive back on your Earth?"

"No."

"I mean, not the exact ones, but others who they passed along the stupid to?"

"No, none of them are," Vel said definitively. "Besides, the Ballooners joined forces with the Fundamentalist Freds, and—"

"Who?"

"The Fundamentalist ... Ah, your Earth didn't play out like that. The Freds were a band of men and woman who all named themselves Fred after the original Fred, who died thousands of years before. He was a spiritual leader, of sorts. He believed that reproduction wasn't violent enough of a process for women, so he preached big-headedness." When Alice was silent below her, Vel correctly interpreted that as confusion. "He said that everyone should have sex with people with big heads to produce big-headed babies that would be more dangerous for women to birth."

"Lemme guess," Alice said, "Fred had a big head."

"One of the largest in fossil records. He practiced what he preached, too. It's estimated that one out of every three people on the planet at the time of my birth was a descendant of Fred."

"I bet you're not. Your head is a normal size."

"Thank you. So anyway, the Fundamentalist Freds and the Ballooners seemed to find common ground in their love for big, round things, and they teamed up. There were a *lot* of them. Easily thirty-five percent of the population, which is all you need for a single group to ruin things for everybody. A third of everyone is apathetic, another third believes something harmfully stupid, and the last third actively opposes the harmfully stupid thing, but sometimes they need a break from the fight, and during that break, the harmfully stupid group, who has nothing better to do and to whom malignant stupidity comes effortlessly, makes moves and passes laws that eventually put them in charge. It's how empires fall."

"And that's how the empire you grew up in fell?"

"How it was falling when I left to fight the war, yes. I tried to fight it on my planet, but I read the signs and enlisted. Left everything I knew behind."

"Were you sad?"

There was a brief silence before Vel spoke. "I was. But I'd been sad for a long time. I fought a losing battle on Earth for longer than most. I wanted to fight a winning battle somewhere. Anywhere."

"Sounds like you made the right decision. You were awarded Queen of the Crabs or whatever, right?"

"Crab Nebula's highest honor of Blood— Well, it doesn't matter now. Yes, I've received awards. And I thought that was what I was after. They made me feel pretty good for a while. I even got a taste of success fighting for the Depot. I didn't know or care to know much about who the Depot was back then. As long as we were winning and I was being recognized for my effort, I was happy." She paused. "No, not happy. Pacified. Or this little thing inside me was pacified, but only temporarily. Then it needed more wins. Then more. And I got those through fighting, so I kept at it.

"I knew all along that it was a game with no end and no winner, but I kept playing it. Even still, it gets old. Maybe that's why I was willing to listen to your orders. I was ready to lose."

"And look where it's gotten you," Alice said cheerfully. "You're free. Free of the Depot, free of the Alliance, free of the fighting."

Vel chuckled humorlessly. "That's what you think you're doing? Liberating us?"

"Duh."

Vel pinched the bridge of her nose. "If you think we can escape any of this, you might be dumber than the Ballooners."

Alice crossed her eyes at the wood grain again. "Guess you'll have to wait and see."

***

Sitting in the gunner's seat on the bridge of *Pythagoras*, Vel set the sight on yet another passing asteroid and fired. It exploded in to three main chunks, which she proceeded to blast into smaller chunks.

Behind her, Alice yelled, "Sooie, piggy piggy!"

It was day twenty-seven aboard the ship on its way to a region of the universe known by most simply as the Farthest Reaches. It was a boring region that was usually only referenced to prove a point. *"I'd rather take a never-ending vacation in the Farthest Reaches than spend another minute being your wife,"* or *"Children who don't listen to their parents get kidnapped and taken to the Farthest Reaches. You don't want that, do you, Dokkun? Then finish your homework before dinner."* The Farthest Reaches, as Alice was discovering, were indeed rather far from everything.

After a low period of no more than a week, wherein Alice had begun to suspect she'd made a terrible decision, she was now enjoying the most fun she'd had in a while.

Dan curled in a tight ball and, covered with a substance much like Vaseline, rolled into the control panel to Vel's left. She hardly spared him a glance before he rolled back toward the center of the bridge.

Alice gauged his speed and trajectory as he rolled closer, then leaped. She had him this time.

But no. Greased hogs had nothing on a greased Pangolian. At least with a hog, she could sometimes get a grip on the hind leg above the ankle joint if the rest of it slipped her. With Dan dressed as he was—naked except for a pair of briefs—the ridges of his armor were tantalizingly close to giving her a finger hold, but not quite enough once the grease was slathered on.

Dan giggled as Alice missed again. He couldn't help it. His adrenaline at being hunted overflowed his system. He peeked out, saw her sprinting at him, then used a leg to propel himself forward before curling tight again. He hit something solid and bounced off, giggling some more.

Caid watched the game from the center of the bridge, occasionally getting passed through by Dan, who was rolling blind, or Alice, who was all tunnel vision.

There was so much to unpack with this game. The need to hunt, the desire to be hunted, the added difficulty of the grease that led to more struggle and greater dopamine rewards. In the end, though, Caid could see that it made both Dan and Alice happier than they'd been in weeks, and it could reset their nervous systems to a more relaxed state after. Then, under the care of their parasympathetic nervous systems, perhaps they would be ready to risk the vulnerability necessary to open up about what was in their hearts.

It will not surprise you to hear that no one had been eager to speak with the crew aide on the long voyage. It did, however, surprise Caid. He would've loved to have someone like him to talk to about the predicament, which was why he spent so much of his days writing in his holographic journal, playing both patient and counselor.

He didn't realize it, but his was the most unhinged behavior taking place aboard the ship.

Dan rolled through him, giggling maniacally, and Alice pursued.

CHAPTER
EIGHTEEN

Boredom is a vacuum. One's brain becomes a small craft floating through the vastness of space, occasionally passing through dangerous asteroid fields, then, if it survives the assault, drifting, drifting, drifting, searching for anything to anchor itself to.

In Homo sapiens, this search is almost inseparable from the hunting instinct. There's a hunger in the search for an escape from boredom that escalates over time. And in the vacuum, all kinds of things can start to look like prey. If the being is especially inclined to hunt, this craving becomes insatiable, and the slightest hint of a diversion becomes irresistible.

It is through that progression that we find Vel crouched behind overturned bunkbeds on the bridge of *Pythagoras,* forty-seven days into a journey toward the Farthest Reaches.

She steadied her breathing, willing her heart rate to lower, her head to clear. It was always best to hunt with a clear mind.

Wiser had been more than generous with his provisions, including big, fuzzy slippers with ample traction that allowed Vel to move about silently without slipping on the layers of grease that now covered almost every inch of floor.

Somewhere in the debris strewn about the bridge, Alice was hiding, too. Vel had never taken the Texan for a woman of stealth, and this newly discovered talent was a pleasant surprise. Vel thrived on tough competition.

A sound. The smallest squeak. Was that a stifled giggle?

Yes, it was. Dan was near, rolling slowly around the obstacle course they'd constructed.

Shooting asteroids had only held her interest for so long. They were too easy to hit. Moving targets, sure, but on predictable trajectories, carried onward by inertia, manipulated only slightly by gravity.

It was no longer enough. She needed more dangerous game.

If she stuck her head out from behind the bunk, Dan might spot her, and he was getting good at evading apprehension.

Really good.

He'd had weeks of practice, and all the better for her, because it kept this challenging.

He knew all of Alice's tricks by now, her tells before she lunged, the way she would toss one of her boots to the other side of the bridge to make him think she was somewhere else. Alice hadn't managed to catch him in days as a result.

But he didn't know Vel's tricks. Not yet. She could still catch him.

A giggle in a slightly different location told her he was

on the move, and she let her instincts take over. No thinking, just movement. Only the hunt.

She rolled out from behind the overturned bed and pounced. But she hadn't anticipated that the only chink in his armor, the space in his tight ball where the crown of his head met the top of his curled knees, would be pressed against the floor. She had nothing to grab hold of, and as she sprang, her arms wide, she already knew it would not be enough. The petroleum jelly on him caused her arms to close with nothing but air between them as he squealed and rolled off. She grabbed at him, hoping to hook a hand under his armor, but he was too quick.

The prey had escaped.

"BLAST IT!" Vel yelled as Dan disappeared behind an overturned weapons rack. She'd have to begin her hunting process all over again, starting with finding a new hiding place.

But before she could, Wiser interrupted. "Farthest reaches of the universe achieved."

At first, nobody onboard understood. The point of their time on the ship had lost out to primal urges of kill or be killed.

Alice was the first to poke her head out of her hiding place. She'd crouched behind a small writing desk on its side that they'd pulled from her and Vel's now-empty bunk room. "Y'all hear that, or am I going crazy?"

Vel blinked a few times, remembered who she was, then said, "If you're going crazy, I'm going crazy too."

Dan uncurled enough to stick his head out, and the jelly made a squelching sound as he did. "There's a distinct possibility all three of us are going crazy."

Alice stood, revealing herself completely. "True. I mean, shit, look at this place."

"We might all be crazy," said Vel, "*and* we might've heard Wiser say we've reached the edge of the universe."

Caid had been meditating in his empty bunk room when the voice spoke, and had immediately headed to meet the others. He stood at the threshold to the bridge, his hands on his hips. "Two things. No, three things. First, enough with the ableist language. Second, enough with gaslighting yourselves. And third, I heard Wiser say it, too. We're here."

Alice glared at him. "Who the hell are you?"

"I'm Cai—" He remembered, looked down at himself, and said, "Oh. No idea."

"You don't even look like a human," she replied.

Curiosity got the best of Dan, and he unrolled the rest of the way to take a gander. "He's a Fronk'gnnok'i. I've only ever met one, and that's not her. I don't know which Fronk'gnnok'i specifically that is, but they have a big tongue dancer scene there, so if Caid is sticking with the trend of famous individuals, he's probably a famous Fronk'gnnok'i tongue dancer."

"Random," said Alice.

"That's the point," replied Dan.

"The point as far as I'm concerned," said Vel, standing and wiping the war paint from her face with her sleeve but doing a good job of smudging it, "is that we're here. The farthest reaches of the universe."

Alice walked to the front window and looked around. "This is it? I don't see any planets or anything. We're just, like, floating in blackness."

"Pardon the interruption, Captain," came Wiser's voice, "but you did not specify anything about a planet. You simply requested that I—"

"I know what I said, you fucking wiseass," she

snapped. "I thought you had artificial intelligence. I thought you could read between the lines. We're trying to escape. To live a life on the lam in somewhere sexy and fun." She huffed exasperatedly. "Keep going. There's gotta be a planet farther out there that fits the bill."

"Error. Cannot go farther."

An orange light flashed on the control panel, and Vel hurried over to attend to it, stepping around a small dresser in her path.

"What do you mean, you can't go farther?" Alice shouted. "This is the universe we're talking about! It's infinite!"

"Correction, Captain," Wiser replied. "This universe is not infinite. You are in a closed system. However, the edge of the universe, like all of the universe, is expanding. I have anchored the ship to it, and we are keeping pace with the expansion at present."

Alice whipped her head around. "Dan! What the hell is he talking about?"

"It's complicated."

"Great, then don't explain it." She looked back out the window, wondered what the next step was, and couldn't come up with one. "Never mind. Explain it."

"We're expanding away from everything all at once in all directions. It's what we usually do, but it's at a slightly accelerated pace at the end of the universe. If we—"

"Changed my mind," Alice said. "Tell me what to do."

"Wiser," said Vel, "unhook us from the edge of the universe."

"Captain, do you confirm these orders?" asked the computer.

"Sure."

"Order confirmed. *Pythagoras* is unhooked from the edge of the universe."

"Phew!" Alice said. "That was a close one." It was an assumption on her part. She had no idea what they were close to, and the fact that she even used the word "close" in this context showed she had zero understanding of universal expansion.

But, of course, everything is relative.

"What now?" Dan asked quietly, deferring to his former captain who only moments before had been hunting him for sport.

"Simple," Alice said. "We keep going. We find somewhere the Depot can't find us."

Vel clenched her fists. "We hit the edge of the universe! If *we* can make it out here on this junker of a craft, the Depot can, too."

The claustrophobic feeling settled in on Alice again. "We'll find a wormhole. Yeah, that's what we'll do. You came through a wormhole, right? We'll find a wormhole and go someplace new."

"There is no better place!" Vel shouted. "This is it!"

"We're not trapped," Alice assured herself. "We're not trapped. There's a way out. A way out of all this!"

Vel stomped over, getting in her face. "There's no way out of this but through. We can't keep running."

"We can. You came in through a wormhole. You came from a different universe. We'll hope into one of those trippy tubes and waterslide into somewhere the Depot doesn't hang out."

"I've never met anyone with less of an understanding about wormholes," Vel spat. "Firstly, they're heavily guarded. *Heavily.* On both sides. Who do you think runs the security on this side, genius? The Depot! We'd never make it past them undetected. You might as well fly us right back to Blerg VFP69 if you're going to do that."

Alice shook her head again and again, attempting to prevent the unwelcome information from making it through her earholes and settling in her brain.

"There's gotta be another way, then. We're not out of options yet. There's always another escape route."

"You've reached the end of the universe, genius!" said Vel. "Maybe you've exhausted your options."

"She's right," said Dan. "There's no other way out."

Vel held her hands out to present Dan, the only sane one, to Alice, the absolutely insane one. "See? Even Dan can tell you. Unless you, I dunno, plan on drilling a hole between universes, there's—"

Alice pointed at Vel. "That! Yes. Let's do that."

"Zap me to quarks!" Vel yelled. "You can't puncture the edge of the universe without *serious* consequences, you ignoramus. You never know what the dimensional composition is in the neighboring universe. It could have twenty-five of them, for all you know, and void swallow anyone who thinks they can guess which dimensions will be dominant. You do *not* want to have the weak nuclear forces turned inside out, and I'll die before I let you introduce a leak like that into this universe, understand? I will blast you down to your subatomic particles before I let you try!"

"Jesus, Susy."

But Vel, it seemed, had had enough. Enough of the running, enough of the stupidity. "Dimensional leaks are deadlier than the Depot could ever be. Deadlier and more destructive. They don't kill life and destroy matter, they *erase* it, turn it into something unrecognizable. They obliterate our single arrow of time, add time dimensions we can't even fathom, and make all history of everything irrelevant and nonexistent. In the truest sense, none of it would've ever happened."

Alice's eyed were wide, and she didn't think she could blink if she tried, because her brain had hooked on to something and wouldn't let it go. "But you're telling me it's something I could do if I set my mind to it?"

Vel lunged, closing her hands around Alice's neck, and the two women went down.

Pinned to the ground, Alice finagled a death grip on Vel's wrists and managed to slip her thumbs underneath Vel's palms to pry them up.

"Stop!" Dan yelled. He rushed forward and threw himself at Vel, knocking into her and toppling her onto her side.

But her grip on Alice's throat remained firm, and Alice gurgled as she, too, was rolled onto her side.

"You're gonna kill her!" Dan hollered, and when it became clear that Vel was hoping for that, he did the only thing he could and brought an elbow down hard between Vel's shoulder blades.

The air went out of her lungs, and it was enough for Alice to finish prying her hands off and roll away, coughing.

"Please!" Caid said, stepping forward. He looked like himself again, or the version of him they were all most used to. "There are always nonviolent options to conflict resolution!"

"*You're* a nonviolent option to … whatever you said," Alice spat. "You're not the one who just got choked by this crazy bitch."

"Oh, *I'm* the crazy bitch?"

Dan scrambled to his feet, looked about ready to jump

between them, then shook his head and folded his arms across his chest to keep his hands from doing anything stupid, like getting him involved again.

"Yeah, *Susy*. Usually the person choking someone else is a crazy bitch."

Vel opened her mouth, then paused. "You know what? You're not the captain anymore. You're nothing. You're an Earthling in space who doesn't know the first thing about how the multiverse works. We're the only people you know anymore, and that means I don't have to listen to you. Wiser doesn't have to listen to you, either. WISER!"

"Yes?"

"I'm the captain now!"

"Confirmation required from previous captain."

"Confirmation denied!" Alice yelled. "Ha! I'm still the captain! Your mutiny failed, Susy!"

"There's no mutiny," Caid said gently, stepping forward. "We're all here for you, Alice. This is merely an interpersonal conflict born from stress. We're under a lot of it right now, but we'll work this—"

Vel stomped her slippered foot. "You bet your *ass* this is a mutiny! One way or another, I'm taking over. Not because I want to, but because you're going to get us all killed. And if I'm going to be killed, it's going to be fighting, not running! Dan!"

Dan's armored back hunched instinctively. "Huh?"

"Do you want to live?"

"Of course I do."

"Then you're with me."

"But ...!" Wide-eyed, he met Alice's fierce and deranged gaze then looked to Vel's murderous one, then, finally, turned to Caid for a little guidance.

Something hardened in the hologram (metaphorically), and he charged forward, stepping between the two women and facing Vel head-on. He pointed a finger in her face, something only someone whose balls could not physically be kneed would try. "You will *not* drag Dan into your conflict. He is a sweet Pangolian who is doing his best. He's loyal to you both, as any good friend is, and it's not his responsibility to choose between the two of you just because *you're* overwhelmed by fear and tossing around ultimatums."

Vel tried to knee him in the balls regardless. "Scream it into the void," she ground out. "You're talking from the cheap seats there, Mr. Hologram. You can't die."

"You think I don't have anything on the line?" Caid replied. "Look what's been happening to me. And Celeste has been experiencing the same. Presumably all of my kind have been experiencing this disruption in their appearance, and what does it mean? You don't think I'm *scared*? For myself? For everyone I know and love? Of course I am! That doesn't mean I get to act out in that fear. I'm responsible for dealing with it."

"And this is me dealing with it," Vel said. "You don't have to like how I'm handling it. At least I'm handling it better than her."

"I'm handling it gracefully as fuck," Alice snapped.

Caid turned to her. "Your fear is going to get us and everyone else in the universe killed."

"Ugh," Alice moaned. "Dramatic much?"

Caid strode over to the window, gazing out. "It's so thick, I can practically smell it. This whole ship reeks with it!"

Alice grimaced. "I've been living off tacos and pizza. Dunno what you expect."

"Fear!" Caid exclaimed. "The whole ship reeks of fear!"

"Ah."

He faced to them. "Fight, flight, freeze, fawn, flop—take your pick! We have it all aboard the *Pythagor*—" A small pop and suddenly he was a purple elephant. Alice stumbled and swatted uselessly as his truck swung through her left side.

Dan peaked out from his protective ball. "What happened?"

"Something random," Alice replied.

Another small pop and Caid was himself. "Wow, that felt majestic. What a beautiful beast to exper—"

Pop.

He was a tube of toothpaste hovering in the air. Alice didn't recognize the brand, though.

Pop.

He was back. "That was alarmingly refreshing," he said. "The word 'wintermint' comes to mind, but that's not a real thing, is it?"

Alice's mouth hung open. "*That's* the most pressing question for you?"

"Something weird is going on," Dan said. "Weirder than normal."

"The randomizations," said Vel, "they're happening more frequently."

Pop.

"I suspect you're right," said Caid as a centaur.

"But why?" Alice asked. "Is something coming?"

Dan considered it. "Caid, are you affected by magnetic forces?"

Pop. He was a squeaking shrub from Trauna now. "Eep-eep eep eep eep eep-eeeep-eep." *Pop.* He was himself again. "Only if you mean charisma," he repeated.

Alice crinkled her nose, staring past Caid through the large viewing window. "Then what could it— The fuck is that?"

Caid became a duplicate Alice and turned to gawk.

"That's not nothing," Vel said, approaching the controls by the window. She squinted ahead. "What is it?"

Dan's superior eyesight made him the first to perceive the details. "It's a cluster of ships. Maybe five crafts. Depot builds, but old ones. Service vehicles. The kind they use to clean up orbital debris when it makes transport impossible. I've also seen that model do construction and deconstruction."

"How the void can you see all that?" Vel muttered, squinting ahead.

"We should probably not approach them," Alice said. "They're Depot."

"Yeah," Dan said, "probably not." But he didn't sound convinced.

"Wiser," Alice said. "What's going on up there?"

"Construction at the edge of the universe."

"They're Depot?" asked Vel.

"Can confirm that the crafts are DeepSLUTs."

Alice chuckled as Dan scratched his head. "But what are service-licensed utility transits doing construction for? And why at the edge of the universe?"

"Nothing good," Vel replied.

"We should probably head away from them," Alice suggested, though her impulse to run was neck-and-neck with her curiosity. "Wiser?"

Vel grabbed Alice's arm to stopped her. Their eyes met. "Not this time, Alice. They're here. At the farthest reaches of the universe. There's nowhere to go. No one to return to. You've lost everything." Without breaking eye contact, she said, "Dan, find us the blasters in this mess."

"Gotcha, Lieutenant."

"And put on some clothes."

Dan shot her a thumbs-up and shuffled carefully across the slick floor to find the blasters.

"Blasters?" said Alice.

Vel nodded, and Alice's lips curved into a sly grin. "Damn. This is some last-stand shit, Susy."

"It is."

Alice grimaced, bracing against the truth. "There's really no more running we can do?"

"There's not."

"So we're doing this? We're seeing what these Depot shitheads are up to, even though it might get us found?"

"We are."

Alice paused, Vel's hand still gripping her arm. The two were toe to toe now. Face to face. Eye to eye.

Alice licked her lips, feeling the breath catch in her lungs. "Are we ... Are we gonna make out?"

"Here." Dan, ignorant to the conversation, thrust two giant blasters between his crewmates.

Alice cleared her throat. "No, of course we weren't." She shook her head to clear it. "Goddamn space celibacy."

Alice gathered her boots from the hunting grounds and slipped them on before addressing the crew. Caid looked briefly like himself. "We gotta face it, y'all. Susy has a point. There's nowhere else to go."

"We already knew that," Dan said. "You were the one—"

"So we're gonna have to fight in one way or another. We're probably gonna die before long, but I promise y'all

I'll make it a good time leading up to that. Now let's go blast those Depot employees to smithereens!"

Dan winced. "Not to be *that* guy, but shouldn't we see what they're up to first? They don't deserve to die just because they work for the Depot. Hell, we worked for the Depot—do we deserve to die?

"Susy almost strangled me," Alice said, pointing a finger. "She seems to think so."

"My point," said Dan, powering through, "is that almost everyone works for the Depot. You can't blame someone for playing the only game around. People need to feed their families."

Alice groaned, leaning her head back. "Uuuugh! I forgot you were a minister of culture. Jesus. Okay. We'll ask questions before we blast people apart." She jabbed a thumb at Dan, addressing Vel. "This fucking guy."

CHAPTER
NINETEEN

"Christ on a cracker. Is that another Bacc'joon?" Alice pointed ahead to the being coming into view through the window of *Pythagoras*.

"Seems to be," said Dan. "But it's a female. Or intersex. Definitely not a male."

The Bacc'joon was standing on a platform atop a tall cherry picker that extended from the edge of a DeepSLUT and ended in what appeared to be completely empty space.

"Reckon it'd be hard to tailor a spacesuit for a male one. Do you add an extra leg or make one leg bigger so he can side-pipe it?"

Having spent her post-collegiate time in Austin, Texas, Alice recognized a construction site when she saw one. This was definitely one. The cluster of DeepSLUTS came in all shapes and sizes. While the Bacc'joon was perched on the boom lift, there was also what resembled a dozer, something that reminded her of a mini oil rig, and one small, caged space that was mostly windows and saws.

Orange cones floated around the whole scene, tethered

together and to the dozer to keep them from floating off. They seemed altogether unnecessary, given the remoteness of this location in the farthest reaches of the universe. Then again, Alice was here, wasn't she? Perhaps this site had more traffic than one would expect.

Caid pressed his hand to the window. It wasn't a hand. It was a paw. (Alice had stopped looking at him if she could help it, since his appearance was a roulette wheel of intergalactic things, and the odds were against any one of those things not being incredibly unsettling.)

"Home," Caid rasped longingly through his gills.

Alice turned to him, saw that he was essentially a bear fish, and regretted it immediately. "That's your home?"

"The edge of the universe, yes." *Pop.*

She risked another look and was pleasantly surprised to find he was now her tenth-grade science teacher, Mr. Foster. The reason she'd ended up studying science.

And, for a moment, she felt like she was home again, too.

"Wait, what is that little thing doing to my home?" Caid demanded.

Alice whipped her head back toward the construction site. Atop the cherry picker, the Bacc'joon held something large and pointy in their arms. And vibrated. "Jackhammering, I reckon."

"That must be it!" Dan declared. "The cause of Caid's condition!"

Caid gasped. "You're right, Dan. They're disrupting the strings. All of them." He turned a concerned eye to the crew, which was all he had, since he'd just turned into an invertebrate cyclops. "If they're disturbing my strings" —*pop* and back to Caid—"then they're disturbing all the closed strings in the universe that correspond to the open ones."

"For the last time," Alice said, feeling the panicked urge to flee return, "like I'm a child. A small one. With a learning disability."

"It's bad," said Caid.

Vel hadn't spoken, only gaped at the scene ahead of them.

Pythagoras floated closer, and Dan was able to identify a second being, who was tethered to a taller cherry picker overlooking the shorter one.

"That's a Noombt," said Dan, as the window ahead of him reflected a deep crease appearing on his forehead.

The Noombt looked to Alice more like her old Furby that would wake up in the night and command her to dance (until her father caught wind, assumed the devil was speaking through it, and hosed it down in the pasture while he called on Jesus to shine down protection; it was the only time Alice ever agreed with her parents about something being possessed).

"We need to get out there and speak with them," Vel said.

Dan nodded, wide-eyed. "Agreed. I have a bad feeling about what they're doing."

"Space walk!" Alice declared, and five minutes later, the three of them stood ready in the cramped airlock, dressed in off-white non-Depot jumpsuits, gloves, and oxygen helmets. Caid joined them as Vel gave the instructions, which were solely for Alice's benefit.

Her voice came through the comms like she was speaking through a can. "Hold on tight to your propulsion board." She lifted hers, which resembled a large metal boomerang. "Tilt to turn, squeeze it tighter to accelerate. Whatever you do, *do not* undo your tether to the ship."

"Why would I—"

"I bet you could find a reason." Vel's attention darted through the airlock window toward the construction site. "I'll do the talking. Whatever you do, don't tell them your real name. There's a chance they are oblivious to the fact that the Depot is looking for a group of fugitives. If they've seen the bulletin, there's no point jogging their memory. Thankfully, one of them is a Bacc'joon and probably not so bright because of it. But the Noombts are sharp. Clever. Cunning. They frequently hire out as spies because of that. Don't let the cute appearance fool you."

Alice's mind flashed back to the night when she could've sworn her Furby told her to "dance for the Adversary," and frowned. "Don't worry about that. I wouldn't trust that guy farther than I could throw him."

Dan blinked, alarm clear in his expression even through the rounded glass of his helmet. "That's *very* far in space. With inertia, you could throw him clear across the universe if nothing knocked him off course. I don't think you should trust him that far, Alice."

Alice sighed wistfully. "I miss Earth, where what I say makes sense."

"I doubt that was ever the case," said Vel. "Are we all ready?"

The port opened, exposing them to the vast emptiness. And then they were off.

Well, Dan, Vel, and Caid were.

Alice squinted at her boomerang, taking in the controls all at once. Then she hit it.

Zipping past her crew with a yeehaw, she nearly

knocked right into the Bacc'joon's mechanical platform before the remembered to tilt the boomerang.

"Who the void are you!" the Bacc'joon shouted.

Vel cursed as she and Dan sped up.

"Hello! We come in peace!" Dan called out, slipping instinctively into diplomacy. "Please excuse my friend. She's not used to the propulsion boards."

"Is something broken?" Vel asked, gesturing toward the edge of the universe.

The Noombt was sparsely dressed, with pants, suspenders, and a clear bubble over his head, through which he narrowed its eyes at Vel. "Who's asking?"

"Me. We were just passing by and noticed you working on it."

The Bacc'joon jackhammered away, sending sparks flying, and the edge of the universe rippled in a dark rainbow against the onslaught. Caid whimpered and turned into a large blue mushroom.

"What in the hole is wrong with him?" said the Noombt.

Alice managed to get her propulsion board under control and circled back around to hover next to Dan.

"He just does that sometimes. It's perfectly normal," Vel lied. "What project are you working on there?"

The jackhammering had ceased long enough for the Bacc'joon to hear the question. "Drill big hole!"

"Fuck me," Alice muttered, not about the content of the response but the way it was delivered. She gawked, ashamed and horrified, at the product of her biological tampering. "Fuck me" was about all one could say in such a situation.

The Bacc'joon's face, which Alice saw better now that it had abandoned the jackhammering and turned to look at them, looked slightly Bacc'nalian but lacked all the cunning of Queen Phet. The eyes drooped like they were melting, and the olive undertones of the skin appeared more jaundiced than radiant. It was still a very round creature, though. That attribute, at least, was recognizable from the Jejoons.

"You're drilling a hole?" Vel said, her voice taking on the deadliness Alice had come to recognize as Vel's expression of fear.

"Who are you with?" snapped the Noombt.

"Who are *you* with?" Alice hurled back.

"We're with The aitch-blasted Depot. You think we do this crap for fun? We're trying to earn a paycheck here. Again, who are you with?"

"We're with the Depot. I'm Captain Luck."

Vel grunted, but showed no other signs of displeasure.

Dan swallowed hard, inspecting Alice for signs of insanity.

Caid turned into the first-place Vitelotte at the 1986 Potato World Championships held in Wimbledon, Kentucky, U.S.A., Blerg VFP69, but no one present knew all that. Alice thought he was a rotten eggplant.

"Never heard of you!" snapped Noombt. "But I can already tell you think you're better than us because of your title. You think because we do grunt work for a living we don't have rich inner lives?"

"GRUNT WORK!" proclaimed the Bacc'joon before it returned to jackhammering wildly at the edge of the universe.

"Would your friend mind taking a quick break?" Alice shouted above the noise.

"She'll do whatever I tell her," the Noombt replied. "But why should I tell her to stop working?"

"We'd like to talk," Alice said. "I think our, uh, missions could help each other out."

"The only help I need is the payment that the Depot is sending to my wife back home. They'll be dead by the time I make it back, and that's half of why I took the job. Keep them off my back, keep them paid, and return home to a dead wife. What could you offer me that's better than that?"

Alice, who by accepting a job with the Depot had herself narrowly avoided taking on what she now understood to be a wife, had no answer.

"Why are you drilling through this universe?" Vel asked. "Don't you know what could happen?"

"I drill!" shouted the Bacc'joon as she continued jackhammering.

"One of two things could happen," said the Noombt. "We could hit on a sweet new universe like ours, which would earn me my Depot bonus, or we could tap into a universe with dimensions nothing like ours, those dimensions would blend to form some weird mixture, and I would entirely cease to exist. In which case, I don't get my bonus, but there's no me anymore, so who cares?"

"You talk about it like it's a fifty-fifty chance of each happening," Vel said, the disgust clear in her tone. "It's not. It's more like a 99.999—repeating, of course—percent chance that the dimensions between any two neighboring but unattached universes are *not* a match."

"Yeah, I get that. It's all or nothing. Literally. So who cares? If it's nothing, there's no me around to care. Never was. This conversation never happened. My first wife never left me. My second never died under mysterious circumstances, and my third never drove me to taking this job. I'm fine with that."

"And you're fine making that decision for everyone else?" Vel demanded.

The Noombt shrugged. "I'm not making the decision. The Depot is."

"But without your labor, they couldn't get it done. You think they'd bring one of their top guys out here to do manual labor? Please. How do you justify playing a part in this? Quintillions of other beings aren't getting a say in whether they live or cease to exist."

The Noombt blew a raspberry, and little specks of spittle dappled the inside of his helmet. "You act like we aren't all doomed for death anyway."

"This is not the same as death!" Vel shouted. "Death leaves things behind. You still exist on the arrow of time after death! You're still remembered. Your atoms exist in the universe forever. You're never gone. But *this*? This is worse than death. When the dimensions change, the atoms break apart. Matter might not even exist anymore. It could just be a thousand time dimensions that take the place of mass in the new reality!"

The Noombt seemed to take that in, then said, "You're awfully worked up about this. You telling me you love everything about your job working for the Depot? It all sits well with you? Come on. Get real. Hey, what's your job, anyway?" The Noombt's eyes darted to the craft behind them. "Since when has the Depot used any of those junkers for its missions?"

"We're covert," Alice replied.

"Not that covert. You introduced yourself to me right away."

The Bacc'joon temporarily lost interest in her jackhammering and turned her attention vaguely toward Alice. "I know you?"

"Uh, nope. Definitely not. We've never met."

"I know you!"

The Noombt's suspicious instincts were officially prickled, and it glared at her. "Why would she know you?"

"Doesn't matter," Alice said. "I'm a high-ranking captain with the Depot, and I order you to stop drilling." There. That would do it.

Noombt scoffed. "No."

"No?"

"Yeah. No. We're going to keep drilling."

Alice turned to Vel, whose expression left no doubt: the drilling, if continued, would erase them all. It had to be stopped.

"Fine," said Alice. "We'll do this the hard way."

She drew her blaster and aimed it at the Bacc'joon.

Dan and Vel drew theirs almost instantaneously, both aiming at the Noombt.

"Oh, come on," the Noombt said, raising his little arms. "We really gonna do this?"

"Of course," Alice said. "You're doing the stupidest thing in the universe. If I was willing to leave the homecoming dance early to make sure Katie Mae didn't end up sleeping with Trev Forsythe, who I *happened* to know had herpes, and thereby give up my chance to romp with *Sam Harzheim*"—she remembered that no one knew anything about Sam—"the hottest guy in Slip'n'Fall, who had a fetish for— Doesn't matter. If I was willing to miss out on *that* to spare a chick I didn't like all that much the possibility of contracting warts, I'm sure as hell willing to blast a hole through y'all's ass to protect the entire universe."

"Noooo!" pleaded the Bacc'joon.

But the Noombt didn't appear similarly concerned.

"Do it. You'd be doing me a favor, frankly. But it won't help."

"Um," said Alice. "Why not?"

"You think this is the only drilling site? Come on. The Depot's located all kinds of thin spots. When we were at the Project: DeepDrill orientation, there must've been three thousand other guys there. Do you see three thousand guys here?"

"Oh balls," Alice muttered, because she did not see three thousand other guys there.

The Noombt's gaze shifted past the strangers over to their ship again. "Here's how I see it. Either you gotta kill us both, which won't do anything, or you gotta kidnap us. Because if you do neither, I'm gonna signal to the Depot that we've spotted some Alliance members parading around as a Depot crew. I have a solid memory. I can describe every one of you. They'll hunt you down, and—"

"FUGIVITVES!" The Bacc'joon jiggled excitedly. "Fugitives, fugitives, fugitives!"

The Noombt's shrewd eyes cut into Alice. "Ah. That makes more sense. I remember hearing something about dangerous Depot fugitives on the loose, but I figured the odds of me running into them at the Farthest Reaches were—"

"Incredibly unlikely," Vel finished for him. "You're right. And the reason unlikely things keep happening is because you're drilling into the edge of the universe, you void-brained hunk of junk. You're messing with the fundamental principles!"

The Noombt rolled his eyes, and an involuntary shudder ran down Alice's spine. "You keep saying that like I care. So, what is it gonna be? Are you gonna kill us or kidnap us?"

Vel shot Alice a cold look that made it clear enough which she'd pick, but Dan had different ideas. "They could have more information about the drilling. If we took them with us—"

"Neither," Alice proclaimed, cutting them off. "We're gonna let you go."

That only increased the suspicion on the Noombt's face, but the Bacc'joon clapped her hands and said, "Yay! We live to drill more!"

"No!" Alice snapped. "You *gotta* stop drilling." She took a different tack, appealing to the Bacc'joon. "What's your favorite thing in the whole world?"

"TOES!"

"Yeah, me too. Toes are great. So fun. Well, if you keep drilling, you'll eventually hit something that will make all the toes in the universe disappear forever."

"NOOO!"

"Yes. Do you want that? Because your friend here wants it. They keep saying they don't care what happens, but what will happen is"—she snapped her fingers as best she could in a spacesuit, which was pretty poorly—"poof, no more toes."

The Bacc'joon gasped then glared at the Noombt. "Why you hate toes, Shirifsks?"

"You daughter of a useless wife," the Noombt cursed at Alice, realizing what she'd just done. Shirifsks turned to the Bacc'joon. "She's lying, Bon Bon. She doesn't know what she's talking about."

But the Bacc'joon was already inconsolable. "WHY NO TOES?!" She tossed away the jackhammer, and it floated through zero gravity until the tether attaching to the workstation pulled taut.

Vel leaned toward Alice. "Far be it from me to tell *you*

to run, but this might be a good time for us to leave if we're not going to kill them."

Alice couldn't help but agree. Before they could, though, Dan spotted something in the distance. The far distance. "Oh void."

And as the Noombt tried to calm their work partner, the thing that Dan had spotted became many things, all of them flashing red and blue.

"Time to skedaddle," Alice declared. "How'd they find us?"

"The Noombt probably had a comm of some kind on it that connected to the Depot or emergency services. I told you they make great spies. Very sneaky." She grabbed Alice's wrist. "Let's get out of here."

Alice looked around, turning carefully on her boomerang. "Where's Caid?"

She spotted a leprechaun floating toward the edge of the universe and was forced to assume that was him. The flashing lights rapidly drew closer as the leprechaun's hands pressed against the edge, sending stunning ripples of light in all directions. The leprechaun kissed the edge of the universe and lingered there. It was the first time Alice had ever seen Caid physically touch something.

Pop. He was himself again. But also not himself. He was glowing, literally glowing, a spectrum of color mixing with his makeup as he kept his eyes closed and pressed his forehead against the edge.

It was so beautiful and overwhelming to see, and Alice had no idea why. Even as the flashing red and blue lights came to a halt and a voice over a speaker told her to freeze and put her hands up, Alice couldn't look away.

Finally, Caid pulled back. He noticed her looking. "Just a little self-love."

"Can we go?"

"Yes. And I think we *should* if you want to live."

"Don't move!" shouted the voice through the loudspeaker.

Caid was still shimmering. "On the count of three, squeeze that accelerator and get to the ship. I'll meet you there. One ... two ..."

On three, he exploded with light like a supernova no one's wife could see coming, and Alice hit it. Blinded by the light, she smashed into the ship to the left of the airlock port. "Christ!"

Vel's hand grabbed her and yanked her in, and then the door slammed shut.

"Wiser!" Vel shouted. "Get us out of here."

"Are you sure you wish to disobey orders from law enforcement?"

"YES," the three of them shouted, and Wiser responded, blasting them forward through space.

Alice yanked off her headgear, gloom setting in. "Allura would never need to be told twice."

CHAPTER
TWENTY

Caid was already waiting for them on the bridge once they changed out of their spacesuits. He appeared refreshed, glowing gently.

"Thanks for, uh, whatever that was," Alice said, thumbing in the direction she assumed they'd come from. "Helped us get away."

"Attention, crew," said Wiser, drawing an involuntary eye roll from Alice. "There are currently fourteen law enforcement ships pursuing us at great speed. Would you like me to head for the nearest space fold?"

Vel rushed to the controls, slipping halfway there on the jelly-slicked floor, and Dan carefully found a seat in the gunner's chair to inspect the panel monitor and grip the gear stick for comfort.

Defaulting to old habits, Vel said, "Incoming. Permission to head for the nearest fold, Captain."

"Yes! Giddy up!"

Still wobbly from her zero-G experience, Alice tumbled backward as the ship zipped forward at max speed. The lubricated floor gave her a ride the rest of the way to the back of the bridge.

She grabbed at the back of her head where it hit the wall. "Oof! Christ!" She rolled to the side, narrowly avoiding being squished by her writing desk. It smashed against the wall, along with most of the other obstacles they'd created.

"They're keeping pace," Vel said, as Alice, bracing on the wall, got her feet under her and shuffled to the captain's chair.

"Are they getting closer?"

"No."

"Then we're golden." Alice buckled herself in as best she could with the jelly covering her hands. She wiped them on her thighs and looked around.

Caid was a plantain.

Dan still had his headset on in the gunner's chair.

Alice frowned. "I guess we shouldn't shoot the cops." Then she remembered the last space police they'd met, Athlathglath'n and Greeps, and added, "Yet."

Always thinking one step ahead, she decided they needed to go faster, so she said, "Susy, can we go any faster?"

"No."

Okay, so that was out. But losing the police was still definitely the goal. "Can we, like, juke them?"

"What does that mean?"

"Fake one way then head another?"

"Are you aware of what radar is?" Vel asked with complete earnestness.

"That's a no, then?"

"Warning," came Wiser's voice. "Energy supply running low. Consider conserving energy."

Vel cursed. "The ship isn't getting as much radiation in the Farthest Reaches. It's expending faster than it's charging."

"How much longer do we have?" Alice asked.

Much to her annoyance, Wiser was the one to answer. "At this velocity, twenty minutes and fifty-eight seconds of ship time."

Vel cursed again. "We're still a half-hour away from the nearest space fold."

The bridge filled with the trill of an incoming comm alert.

"Should I answer it, Captain?" Vel asked.

"Depends. Who is it?"

Dan scoffed. "Who is it? Who do you think it is? The void-blasted police!"

Taken aback by his attitude, Alice said, "Oh, well, obviously. Don't answer it."

"I think we should answer it," Vel replied.

"Fine. Answer it." Alice slouched back in her chair, muttering, "Why even ask me?"

"I'm answering it in audio only. They won't be able to see us, and we won't be able to see them."

Alice's brain ran through an inventory of every alien she'd met and decided that the odds favored this being a good thing. Too many beings looked like gummy worms with loose hair stuck to them.

Vel accepted the communication, and the voice echoed through the bridge. "Police. Stop running. We will apprehend you eventually. Your penalty will be less severe if you cease evading arrest."

Dan and Vel looked to Alice.

She didn't like this guy's tone. "If you don't like it, maybe you should stop chasing us. Ever thought of that?"

"We … Huh?"

Alice smirked. They clearly hadn't thought of it.

"We will not stop pursing you," the voice replied. "Surrender, fugitives."

Time and energy were running out. They were doomed to be caught and arrested. Were there Miranda rights in outer space? Habeas corpus? Doubtful.

If apprehension was inevitable, compliance was probably smart. At least the patrollers might be less pissed off. That would bode well for her and her friends. Some sort of leniency, maybe even compassion.

But then what? Lifelong imprisonment? Death?

Alice unbuckled herself then skated across the floor to the control panel, standing shoulder to shoulder with her lieutenant. In front of them, the round comms button flashed blue to indicate that the call was still active.

"Sure, we'll surrender," Alice said, struggling to suppress a grin. "After you suck my dick!" She slammed her hand down on the blue light, ending the call.

Dan ripped his headset off and stared wide-eyed at his captain.

"I don't have a dick," she clarified.

"That's not why I'm freaking out!"

But beside her, Vel chuckled darkly. "Oh man. We're *doomed.*"

"Not yet, Susy. We still have—"

The ship lurched, and Alice grabbed on to the control panel to avoid sliding on her ass for the second time in the last few minutes. "They're shooting at us!"

"What did you *think* would happen?" Dan demanded, jamming the headset back on and getting the closest of the police crafts in his cross hairs. "Waiting on orders to return fire."

"It'll cost us too much energy," Vel advised, picking herself up off the floor and wiping her greasy hands on her stomach (she hadn't grabbed hold of anything quickly enough).

"Hold fire," said Alice. "I have a better idea anyway."

"You do?" said Dan and Vel.

"I knew you would," said Caid, no longer a plantain.

Alice turned to face her team, her hands braced on her hips. All eyes were on her. "We're facing two major problems: the fuzz and the drilling, right? We can't outrun the cops, and we can't stop thousands of drillers on our own. We also can't escape any of this, *apparently*." She glared at Vel as if it were her fault they lived in a closed universe. "So we need help. We need to call in the Alliance."

"On it." Vel pressed her hand to the controls and spoke a single word. "Chorus."

Alice and Dan looked at each other.

"Uh, Susy?"

"It's a word they gave me. If I wanted to call them, I needed to broadcast the word 'chorus.' Let's hope the Alliance really is scattered everywhere and there's someone close by."

"And you're sure they'll—"

An armada appeared out of blackness ahead of them.

"Oh damn. Sweet!" Alice fist-pumped.

And then the armada began firing. The blasts ripped nail-bitingly close to *Pythagoras*, and Alice felt her entire body pucker. She shuffled quickly but carefully back to her chair and buckled up again.

"They're not shooting at us," Vel assured her. "They're firing at—"

Alice saw the flash a second before it made impact

with their ship. The jolt tossed Vel two yards, and the jelly took her the rest of the way to the wall.

"They're *yokels*, Susy! Not soldiers!" The lieutenant had clearly never been to a Friday night football tailgate during rattlesnake season. If she had, she'd know that just because everyone was firing at the same enemy didn't mean no one lost a foot in the process.

Vel stayed low, army-crawling to her own secure chair.

"Wiser," Alice yelled, "get us out of the line of fire, please. Burn all the energy if you gotta."

"If we burn all the energy—" Dan began, but Alice cut him off.

"We don't need it, Dan. This is it. Y'all were right. There's nowhere left to run to. And even if there were, I think we gotta stay. *I* gotta stay. I gotta fight." An explosion in front of them blasted bright light through the bridge. "Not just for the things I could lose or the things y'all could lose, but for the things we've already lost." She thought once more about the A that Brenda would create in her lattes. A for Alice. *Brenda, Brenda, Brenda* ... "Let's keep what we still have of them. Let's protect them on the arrow."

"And in our hearts," Caid added.

Alice gagged. "Dammit, Caid. You just— Ugh. Now it's sappy."

"Yeah, you ruined it," Vel said.

And then the crew settled in, clear of the line of fire, and watched the Alliance fleet drive the red and blue lights off into the deep abyss of space.

CHAPTER
TWENTY-ONE

Throughout her public school years, Alice had been summoned to the principal's office more than her fair share of times, yet the sense of impending dread as she walked the halls toward the latest dressing-down never faded. Sitting in the small conference room onboard the spaceship *Paradox* with the Alliance's president and top-ranking officials, Alice felt that same heaviness in her stomach.

It was clear to Alice who the principal was in this situation. President Leviathan glared at her across the table.

This time, Alice had two boys with her. And one terrifying girl. And instead of her mother and father providing backup for the principal, there was a rebel space captain, a hologram, and a cactus guy.

The two groups positioned themselves on opposite sides of the oval conference table, and Alice thought she could really use a cold beer. She'd almost died, after all. That deserved a little booze.

"I have two questions," Leviathan began. "First, why did you go straight to the Farthest Reaches the moment we gave you a ship?"

Alice tried not to chuckle at the slow pitch. She would lie, obviously, but this one was almost too easy. This lie wrote itself. The only problem would be if one of her friends decided to air a guilty conscience and rat her out. "You saw Celeste changing randomly, right? She couldn't control it."

Leviathan nodded.

"And I know you saw that the same was happening to Caid, as well."

"Yes. His well-timed switch got us out of a tight spot with the patrollers."

"Exactly. So that got me to thinking"—lie number one—"that maybe there was something going on, cosmically speaking, that was causing that. And what affects a hologram?"

Leviathan narrowed her eyes but didn't answer.

"The edge of the universe. Caid mentioned it when he first explained what an organic hologram was to me. Something was messing with his, uh, strings or whatever."

Celeste shared wide-eyed concern with her counterpart across the table, who nodded solemnly.

"Then there was all the random stuff happening. Remember Dan's strange jitters? Random. And that big squid in the sky on Loqqen? Random!"

"It makes sense," Astra said, sparing Alice from having to tie the two bits of evidence together by explaining all the multiple dimension stuff. "Both could come from the same cause. I'm surprised we didn't put it together sooner."

"Eh, don't beat yourselves up." Alice waved her off. "Not everyone can be as smart as our crew." She grinned at Vel, who did not grin back. She was too busy keeping her eyes fixed on her parallel double.

"And what did you find at the Farthest Reaches?" Leviathan asked. "Did your theory prove correct?"

"Oh, right! You didn't see the asshole Furby. So, yes, our theory seems correct. We found the Depot drilling into the edge of the universe."

President Leviathan shot to her feet. "Where? I need coordinates. We need to stop that before—"

"We know," Alice said, impatiently. "It's bad. Very bad. And I'm sure the coordinates are logged on Pythagoras. Wiser probably can't wait to report them to you." She rolled her eyes. "But here's the deal, Lev: the drilling site we found is only one of thousands. We have a massive problem on our hands. One so big that I think you should drop all suspicion of us and focus on the task at hand, ya know?"

Leviathan stared at the air over Alice's head, her eyes wide, then she turned to Astra. "Can you get the word out? Everyone deserves to know. As many of the members as you can."

Astra nodded and left the room.

"What I would like to know," Alice began, "is how the hell y'all got to us so fast. It took us weeks of ship time to get there. Then you show up in a second? Did we take the goddamn scenic route or what?"

"We were following you," Lilqua'tartian spat, and Leviathan shot him a stern look for speaking out of turn.

"It's true," she said, addressing those across the table. "We were following you. We weren't sure where you were going, so we wanted to keep a safe distance to allow you to go incognito, as you requested, but be available for reinforcements, should you need them. As it turns out, you needed them."

"We didn't trust you," Lilqua'tartian added, and a muscle in Leviathan's jaw visibly clenched.

But Alice only grinned at him. "We proved you wrong, didn't we?"

Lilqua'tartian grunted in a way that made it clear that was still to be seen.

"Are you still up for leading the Alliance?" the current president asked.

Alice shrugged. "I could do that, I guess."

"That's the spirit," muttered Lilqua'tartian. "A true-born leader."

"You'll need to address them," Leviathan continued. "They need to hear from you. There are plenty traveling with us now. I can arrange for us to gather on the bridge of *Paradox*. It's the largest ship of the fleet and has enough space to fit everyone, I believe. Would you do that?"

Alice crinkled her nose. "Like a speech?"

"Yes." Leviathan paused. "I thought that was clear when I said you'd address them."

Shrugging, Alice said, "Yeah, I could make that happen."

How many people could it be, anyway? She'd never once prepared ahead of time for her high school speech class, and she'd aced it. She liked to believe that was because she knew how to think on her feet and not because Mr. Larson, who was later arrested for inappropriate relationships with no fewer than nine freshman girls, had been grooming her.

Vel chimed in, "You said you had two questions. What was the second?"

"Ah," said Lev, remembering. "Right. Any idea why the crew who I sent over to collect your things reported that the bridge of Pythagoras was … greasy?"

CHAPTER
TWENTY-TWO

Alice stood at the center of the gathering aboard the largest of the Alliance's ships. No fewer than one hundred and fifty beings of various shapes, sizes, and smells had crammed themselves into the space to hear what the Texan had to say. Around her rose and fell waves of belching and gurgling from loose esophagi. President Leviathan had done her part by assembling the assembly, and now all were waiting for Alice to speak.

While a part of her wanted to click the heels of her Texas-flag boots three times while chanting, "There's no place like home," her journey to the Farthest Reaches had allowed her mind the space-time to accept that there might be no place like home, but there was also no more home. Everything she knew on Earth was gone. She may as well call it Blerg VFP69 like everyone else did. There *was* no place like home. Not even her home planet.

And if that was how it shook out, then it was game time.

Alice loved game time. She imagined that the Friday night lights of the tiny Slip'n'Fall Farm Supply Stadium shone on her instead of the uniform glow of the bridge of *Paradox* and all those eyes and gooey eyelike things glistening at her now transformed to the gazes of people from her hometown who said she wouldn't amount to nothin' if she didn't get right with Jesus. She never had, but look at her now!

Time to deliver.

"Thank you for coming to our aid," she said, addressing the onlookers. "Your assistance with *Pythagoras* allowed us to investigate a growing suspicion of ours related to the random events taking place more and more frequently. It's as we feared. The existence of, well, *everything* is at risk. Our intel is that the Depot has at least three thousand workers drilling at the edge of the universe."

A gasp rose from the crowd, and though she hated to admit it even to herself, it was the first time Alice herself felt how big of a deal this was.

"Yeah," she said. "Pretty fucked up, huh?"

"They'll erase us all!" someone shouted.

"No shit," Lilqua'tartian barked back. "Shut up and let her finish."

She offered a small bow of appreciation to the cactus. She might actually like him before all was said and done.

"All of us have chosen to leave what we love behind to pursue a life in space. You were probably aware starting out that by the time you returned home, if you ever did, what you knew and loved would be lost to time. I didn't know that. No one told me. And now it's all gone.

"I never had a choice. But I have one now. We all have one now. We can keep all that we've lost alive, but *only* if we work together and unite to stop this drilling. The

Depot is playing an all-or-nothing game that we didn't agree to, and it's betting the whole-ass farm on it.

"I'm gonna be straight with you: I don't give a shit what your position is on third-party selling. I really don't. Frankly, I struggle to even grasp the basic concept. But what I do understand is that if the Depot taps into a new universe with different dimensions from ours, there will be no third-party selling. There will be no first-party selling. Or, uh, second-party selling? There will be no selling! There will be nothing. No one. Since ever and forever." She shot a sideways glance at Vel, who indicated with a small nod that she was still getting it all correct.

"So, sure, I'll be your Texan. I dunno why y'all are so hung up on that, but if it does it for you, then I'm in. But you gotta follow my lead. No more infighting. This is bigger than that. This is everything. Remember what you're doing it for. Remember everything you've lost. Because we're going to fight, and some of us are probably gonna die. But if you die, the rest of us will keep fighting for you, because you'll have become something else we've lost. Something more, something worthy of remembering. Even if you survive this, even if we win, one day you'll die. I want you to still exist in this moment, at this point on the arrow of time. Always. *I* don't want to be erased. I kinda like this moment. I want it to keep existing for all of time, don't you?"

She saw adamant nodding all around her, and the general belching had increased from excitement, but that wasn't good enough.

"Do you want to be erased?"

"*No!*" came a few of the voices.

A hard-to-rouse crowd, eh? She went for the easy win. "Do you want the Depot to win?"

"*No!*" came even more voices.

"And do you want every happy memory you've ever had to be erased?"

Even louder now: "*No!*"

"So are we gonna fight?"

As the bridge erupted into cheers, Alice wiggled her toes excitedly in her boots.

She'd won them over, kept their attention, maybe even inspired them.

Hot damn, she thought, wishing Jacob could see her now.

Then she remembered that she was technically unemployed again and felt suddenly grateful that he only existed in her memory.

"We're gonna fight 'em, and we're gonna win. And I'll gladly lead you every step of the way, because if there's one talent I was born with, it was giving folks hell!" She grinned, remembering her resilience against those exorcism attempts. "But I'm warning you right now: it's gonna get weird. Causing trouble always does. Are we ready to get weird?"

The initial cheer had already died down, and the murmur of agreement, the heads and headlike things nodding and wobbling, was no longer enough for her.

"I said, are we ready to get weird?!"

A chorus of voices broke out once more, punctuated with loud pops of esophageal sounds.

She imagined the cheerleaders at her high school seeing her now, leading a real cheer. Those girls were all dead now.

She did now feel sad about that.

If she was going to end this on a high note, now was clearly the time, so she got them started on a chant of

"Weird! Weird! Weird!" conducting them with a fist pump each time as she cut through the crowd and made her way to a side room.

Her trusty crew met here there shortly, along with Quark Leviathan.

"Not bad. I didn't know you had it in you," she said, eyeing Alice approvingly down her perfectly carved nose.

"I did," said Dan, beaming. "I knew she had it in her."

Alice clapped him on the back. "Thanks, bud."

"It's time to talk about the first step," Leviathan added, cutting Alice's praise session short. "What do you need from me?"

Alice nodded. She'd thought about it before her speech. Always thinking exactly one move ahead. And the next move was so, so obvious. "I need a ship with Allura 4000."

Leviathan's mouth fell open. "That sex tourism operating system?"

"That's her! She saved us, if you've forgotten. She didn't have to let our escape pods leave, but did. You know why? Because she was smart enough to know that Daddy knows best."

At a loss for words, Leviathan turned to Vel, who shook her head, discouraging any further questions.

"Can you get me a ship with her on it?" Alice asked.

Leviathan blinked. "Yes, I'm sure I can. No one wants—"

"Good. Because I can't do this without her. None of us can. I'm no good at guessing the future, but there's one thing I know. Like I said out there, if we stand any chance of winning against the Depot, we're gonna need to get deviant. Get me Allura 4000, then we'll give the Depot dickheads hell."

ALICE LUCK CONTINUES...

Thanks for reading.

There is plenty more of the Alice Luck Space Adventures on the way.

If you want me to send you an email when the next one is out, go to www.hclairetaylor.com/hi to sign up for notifications.

-H. Claire

ABOUT H. CLAIRE TAYLOR

H. Claire Taylor is the author of the Jessica Christ comedy series about God's only begotten daughter as well as the Kilhaven Police series about a rookie human cop getting his ass kicked in a city of paranormal beings.

She lives in Austin, Texas, with her husband, John, who laughs at all her dumb jokes and is generally the love of her life.

Claire is also the owner of FFS Media, through which she publishes the books she writes under her four pen names.

instagram.com/claireorwhatevs
amazon.com/author/hclairetaylor
bookbub.com/authors/h-claire-taylor

BOOKS BY H. CLAIRE TAYLOR

The Alice Luck Space Adventures

Lucky Stars (Book 1)

Cluster Luck (Book 2)

Ship Out of Luck (Book 3)

The Jessica Christ Series

The Beginning (Book 1)

And It Was Good (Book 2)

It's a Miracle! (Book 3)

Nu Alpha Omega (Book 4)

It is Risen (Book 5)

In the Details (Book 6)

The End is Her (Book 7)

The Kilhaven Police series

Shift Work (Book 1)

Same Old Shift (Book 2)

Shift Out of Luck (Book 3)

Deep Shift (Book 4)

Wimbledon, Kentucky

See all at www.hclairetaylor.com

Find more books at www.ffs.media